DANCE WITH DARKNESS

DEIIRA SMITH-COLLARD

An Urban Paranormal Thriller

A Novel

By

DeiIra Smith-Collard

Copyright © 2019
DeiIra Smith-Collard

Published by DeiIra Smith-Collard

Prologue

October 31, 1994

The balmy muggy wind fluttered over her body as she ran through the dark dank street. The soft pitter-patter of her bare feet carried her through the abandoned roads as blood trickled down her thighs. Her heavy labored breaths escaped her lips as pain soared through her body in pulsating waves, leaving her almost incapable of concentrating on anything else.

Keep Going... Keep Going... Keep Going

The words replayed over and over in her head as she willed herself to move faster. She was running out of time.

She belongs to us. The ominous voice continually called out to her, claiming her child as their own. The words felt like a tightening noose around her neck, sucking all the life from her. Her heart palpitated, creating an erratic symphony of chaotic beats.

You will upset the balance, all debts must be paid. The wind now carried the whispers of her ancestors, warning her, but the fear that her baby's life would turn out worse than her own pushed her forward. They always called it a gift but to her, it was an eternal curse. Her powers were great and she had been used, but her child was special, and with such powers would forever be a target.

Any date but this date, she had prayed that it would skip a generation, but her prayers had fallen on deaf ears. Her daughter had been born, with the mark and on the date. She would be the next in line to carry on the legacy and fulfill the prophecy.

She looked over her shoulder as she ran and then down at her child. The child she had birthed only hours ago. She had only the first six hours after birth to perform the ritual, after that she wouldn't be able to stop it. On the seventh hour, the cycle would begin, and her baby's life would never be her own.

She is ours

The menacing voices again floated through the night air, carrying with it an ominous feeling. Her heart thumped against her chest as she looked behind her. She could feel it getting closer and closer to her. So close the hairs on the back of her neck stood at attention. Again, she glanced over her shoulder this time using her connection to the elements to track it's proximity to her.

What she was about to do was blasphemous to those who came before her. Her talents and the talents that she knew would be passed on to her child were considered sacred gifts bestowed upon her by God. Altering or changing his will was a slap in the face to the LOA who had interceded in prayer to God to bless her ancestors.

Her legs burned as she continued to run through the streets, desperately trying to get to the haven of the graveyard. It was there she knew she could complete the spell and make sure her child was never used. She could ensure her child would never see the evils she had grown up with, and she would never be anyone's sacrifice.

The child and the bag she carried was heavy in her weakened arms, but she continued on. Her eyes closed as she turned through the streets. Even without sight, she could see. When she closed her eyes and listened her second vision was heightened, seeing both the seen and unseen elements of the world.

His spirit was close behind her, black and ominous it meant her no good. The tall shadowy figure was sent to capture her and take her child away. She shook her head furiously, she would die before she allowed harm to come to this child.

Finally, reaching her destination she ran into the graveyard searching for her location. Raised in the religion of Voodoo, but a practitioner of Hoodoo she would harness the power of magick to protect her child. She rushed inside searching for the grave of Marie Laveau, her grandmother's, grandmother's grandmother. Only the select few knew of her rich cultural history. For years her family profited from the lessons passed down from generation to generation, and then she came. She was told she could be as powerful as Grandmother Marie had once been. She looked down at her daughter. Her beautiful child and tears slipped from her eyes. There were many things about her gifts that could be used for good, but there were many more that could mean complete ruin for the child.

She knew there existed a world beneath the world. One where good and evil fought tirelessly for control, a world that was not bound by the rules of fairness, but of power. There was a constant battle between good and evil and one could be easily lost in a world like that, as she had once been. She exhaled and focused on her mission.

Don't

The wind whipped past her ears carrying the message. She ignored the voices that whizzed past her. Reaching the tomb, she reached into her bag with her free hand and pulled out a glass bottle of salt, blessed and pure she would need its protection. She opened the spout and enclosed herself and her child in the circle. After she completed the circle, she sat down the bag she carried with her. Now confident she would be protected, she laid her baby in the center and pulled out a piece of paper and three satin ribbons, blue for healing, black to repel dark energy, and white for positivity and protection.

Her fingers worked hastily braiding the ribbon together, her baby's gentle cries fueled her motivation. She looked down at her baby for a brief moment, staring into the child's misty gray eyes.

"You will have the life I never had." She spoke. After finishing the braided ribbon she sat it to the side. Her heart drummed inside of her chest, beating to its own chaotic rhythm.

She removed her baby's hospital band and placed it next to the ribbon. Slipping her hands back into the bag she carried with her, she pulled out a small bracelet with the name, *Maya Pussaint* engraved in the gold, she needed to give her child a piece of her history, even if it was in name alone.

Lastly, she pulled a piece of paper she had prepared, her petition. She took the hospital bracelet and wrapped it in the paper, folding it and folding it again. She moved faster, she could feel the shadowy figures at the gates of the cemetery, but her protection circle held them at bay. After the paper was folded she began to wrap it tightly with the ribbon. Performing manipulative magick such as this was frowned upon, but she was desperate to protect her.

She chanted as she continued to tightly wind the cord, binding her powers and her second sight so that the child could have a normal life. She securely tied the ends of the ribbon in a knot completing the binding.

Knowing that a sacrifice would have to be made for the Loa to assist her she reached inside of her bag and began to pull out her offering. She placed to her left black coffee, cigars, and then she pulled out a bottle of rum steeped with twenty-one of the hottest peppers and poured it into a small glass. Her offering was tailored to one specific Loa, it was for the Baron. She would need the blessing of Baron Samedi, she would not be successful without his permission, and she hoped he would hear her pleas and his love for children would help her save her own.

Next, she pulled out a small knife. The handle was ornate with gold and silver entwined. She stared down at the dagger and at her child. The voices in the wind had quieted. She could feel the watchful eyes of the spirits on her but nothing was audible.

"Maya, you will be protected. I give myself for you." She uttered and then plunged the knife into her heart. The warm blood spilled from her body as she fell beside her daughter. As her vision dimmed her sight became clearer. There would be a couple to raise her, she would be taken far away. She would be okay. A smile spread across her face as death took her. She had done it, her daughter would be protected.

The wind gushed through the quieted graveyard carrying with it the ribbon binding and her one mistake. A spell must be specific and although she had been successful, it would not be lasting.

Chapter One

"I can't believe they're gone," Maya said as she turned to face her sister. Tears pooled in the corners of her eyes as the realization of her parents' death hit her. Her parents had been her lifeline, and the thought of living without them was earth-shattering. Life as she knew it would never be the same and that one thought pained her to her core.

She scanned the house as they walked inside of their parents' home. The air carried the faint smell of their scent. Their mother's cooking mixed with their father's cologne wafted softly through the small space. Her heart ached. She noticed her sister had not spoken since they left their parents' funeral. The day had been exhausting and emotionally draining. Watching her parents being lowered into the ground had knocked the wind out of her and she knew if she felt this way, then Jeniva's fragile feelings were shattered to pieces. She turned her attention towards her baby sister waiting for her to respond. There was nothing.

Jeniva stood frozen in the entryway, hugging her small willowy frame. Her pain was a slow simmer that had just begun to boil. For days after, she had convinced herself that her parents would walk through the door at any moment. Somehow, she tricked herself into believing that they were alive and the hospital had just made a mistake. Jeniva looked up at her sister, her eyes were ladened with sorrow. The contrast between the two of them always took people by surprise. Jeniva was a miniature version of their mother, all of 5'2 and as thin spaghetti, but Maya was every bit of 5'10 and curvy.

"Niva, did you hear me?" Maya walked towards her sister and wrapped her arms around her, embracing Jeniva. Maya sensed she would fall apart at any moment. Jeniva buried her head in Maya's bosom and allowed the dam to burst. She hadn't allowed herself to shed one tear. Her emotions rolled between anger and denial, she was stuck in a continuous loop of grief.

"I would give anything for them to be here right now," Jeniva whispered through her grief-stricken sobs. She was slowly moving into her bargaining stage. The desire to have them back was great, and if she could honestly make a deal with God to have them back she would.

Maya searched for the right words to say as she closed her eyes and exhaled. She wanted nothing more than to ease the pain her sister was feeling, the pain that she was feeling, but she knew there was nothing she could do that would begin to take away the hurt they felt. She released her grip on her sister and led her to the couch.

"We are going to be okay, it will take time. Why don't you lay down and I will make us some tea?" *A warm drink to wash your worries away.* She smiled as she recalled her mother's voice. Jeniva took a seat on the sofa and Maya headed towards the kitchen.

She lit the stove and placed a kettle of water on the pilot and waited for the whistle. As she slid into her mother's chair at the breakfast table, she noticed the plastic bag the hospital had given her with her parents' belongings. The ache in her heart grew stronger as she reached for the bag, knowing that the contents of this package were some of the last things they touched.

Her father's watch was the first thing she was drawn to. Its shattered face seemed to capture her attention. It had been a gift from her mother and he had proudly worn it for years. Maya's fingers trailed the lines of the watch slowly circling around the cracked glass.

She closed her eyes, remembering his presence. She could almost feel him. She exhaled and a wave of heat rushed over her. Maya's heartbeat quickened as flashes of light pulsed through her closed eyelids. She tried to open them but could not. Her mouth became bone dry as she struggled to swallow. The smell of smoke invaded her nostrils as visions of her parent's black Mercedes sedan crept into her thoughts.

She could see a cloud of black smoke enveloped the car as it sped uncontrollably down the highway. Her father's panicked face flashed then his desperate attempt to gain control of the vehicle. Her breathing intensified, she smelled the burning rubber of the tires and the stench of burning metal.

The whistling tea kettle jolted her and she dropped the watch releasing her from its grasp. Maya looked around the room as she gripped the edge of the table, unsure of what was happening. To her, it felt as if she was losing her grip on reality.

What the hell was that? She thought to herself as she slowly moved her chair away from the table and walked towards the stove. She turned off the gas and attempted to shake the eerie thoughts that had just overtaken her mind. She slowly dipped the tea bags she had opened, steeping the chamomile tea for the two of them. She needed the soothing tea just as much as her sister did.

Quietly walking through the house, she moved back towards the living room where her sister lay sleeping on the sofa. She sat her sister's cup of tea down on the coffee table and took a seat on the couch across from her sister. She sipped slowly as she tried to push thoughts of what just happened out of her mind. Her phone rang, giving her a much needed reprieve from her thoughts.

"Hello," she spoke softly.

"Maya?"

"Yes, speaking. How may I help you?" She hadn't recognized the number but with everything that was needed to plan her mother and father's funeral she had almost become accustomed to answering unknown numbers.

"This is Lance Sloan, your parents' estate lawyer, I was calling to schedule a time for you and your sister to come in for the reading of the will. I know it's sudden but could you guys manage to come in on Monday?" His tone was professional but compassionate.

Even though Maya had no desire to discuss her parent's will and estate she knew it was something that had to be done, and as the oldest, she knew that it was something that she would have to take the lead on.

"Yes, we will be there. What time is good for you?" She asked.

"Ten would work perfectly if you guys can manage." Attorney Sloan responded.

"We will see you then."

Maya responded and then disconnected the call. Her sister's soft breathing calmed her. She dreaded the road ahead of her, but as much as she did she knew that she was going to have to be strong for her sister. Maya reached for her mother's throw blanket and inhaled it before wrapping it around her body. She drifted off to sleep dreaming she was wrapped in her mother's loving embrace.

Chapter Two

aya and Jeniva rode in silence as Maya steered the car towards the exit to the lawyer's office. Jeniva hadn't said much of anything and Maya didn't know how to break the silence. Rather than pressure her to talk about what she was feeling, Maya allowed her the time she needed to open up. She turned into the parking lot and slid into an open spot.

"Let's get this over with," Jeniva muttered. Even though her voice was barely above a whisper, Maya was happy to see her slowly breaking her silence.

"I don't understand why I had to be here for this." Jeniva picked at her nails, speaking without ever looking up at Maya. Maya closed her eyes, putting distance between her immediate thoughts and the words she would speak. She understood where her sister was coming from and she didn't want to say anything that would hurt her sister or make her retreat back into her shell when she was just starting to open up. If Maya was being completely honest with herself, she didn't want to be here either, but it was necessary.

"We both have to be here, we are both named in the will. We need to do this together." Maya reached towards Jeniva, grabbing her hand and squeezing slightly in an attempt to calm her. "Let's just get it done."

Jeniva shook her head and opened the car door to step out. Maya was trying to stay strong for her younger sister, being the oldest she had always been protective of Jeniva. On the outside, she was a rock, but on the inside, she was falling apart. Maya felt she was too young to deal with all of these things. She was just a few days short of being twenty-five and now all of a sudden her entire life had changed.

They entered the building in silence and got on the elevator. Jeniva looked at Maya fighting back the tears that were threatening to surface. She briefly wondered if Maya felt as empty without them as she did.

"I do," Maya said.

"You do what?" Jeniva eyes narrowed as she stared at Maya.

"You asked me if I felt empty," Maya turned her attention back to the elevator, their floor should be coming up next.

"No, I didn't!" Jeniva's lip curled upward as the point of her nose dipped. "I didn't say anything."

The elevator dinged alerting them to their stop and they exited. Maya cut her eyes towards Jeniva. She had clearly heard her ask the question, so why was she denying it now. Maya stopped before they walked through the glass doors into the lawyer's lobby.

"Niva, it's nothing to be ashamed of. The way you are feeling is normal, as long as we are honest with each other and are here for each other we can get through this together." Maya finished. Jeniva stared blankly at Maya, her eyes void and absent of any emotion, then she turned her attention to the glass doors leading to the attorney's office. Maya stood motionless, waiting for Jeniva to respond but she didn't say anything. Jeniva resumed her walk to the glass door, interrupting Maya's thoughts. She decided to let it go. They walked into the lobby and Maya headed to the front desk to check-in.

"Hello, My name is Maya St.James, my sister and I are here to see attorney Sloan."

"Good morning Ms. St. James, Mr. Sloan is expecting you, please have a seat in the waiting area, and he will call you in shortly."

Maya shook her head and sat in the empty seat next to her sister. Maya and Jeniva were the only two in the waiting area, it was only moments before their names were being called. The perky lady at the front desk stood and led them to the back of the office.

"Mr. Sloan, this is your ten, Ms. Maya and Jeniva St. James."

"Hello ladies, please have a seat." He motioned his hand towards the two open chairs in front of his desk. Both of them took a seat but said nothing. Neither of them honestly knew what to say. This was foreign to both of them. Attorney Sloan looked at both women with sympathy, the deep lines etched in his face exposed the compassion he felt for the sisters. These matters never got any easier for him. Any reading of the will after death so tragic was never painless and he knew the information he was going to have to deliver would be even more difficult than usual.

"Uhmm Hmm," he cleared his throat. An awkward silence had fallen over the room, but he knew things were going to have to move forward.

"The reason I called you ladies in today is for the reading of your parents' will. Your parents had very specific instructions regarding their desires in the event of their untimely death."

Jeniva started to softly sob. She pressed her lips together, fighting back the sounds that were attempting to escape her lips. She had worked so hard to be in control, but the weight of what was happening was just too much for her. Maya reached for her hand as Mr. Sloan handed her tissue.

"Okay, we are ready," Maya said, attempting to gently nudge this meeting along. She was far too emotionally drained to even pretend as if she wasn't ready to get this over with. Her parents' belongings meant nothing to her. She would much rather have them back. The attorney shook his head and proceeded to read their parents' last will and testament.

The pair listened intently, neither of them surprised. They knew their parents would always be fair. Growing up their parents had made it very clear that they were to take care of each other, share with each other, and love each other. For them, this moment would be no different. Mr. Sloan finished reading and placed the document on his desk and looked above the rim of his glasses at the girls.

"Do either of you have any questions?" Both of them shook their heads in unison, bouncing their hair from side to side. Anxiety rushed through Jeniva's body. The heaviness within these walls crushed her emotionally and hearing her parents' last will and testament seemed to finalize everything. This room made everything official for her and she just wanted out and away from this space.

"Thank you, Mr. Sloan. If we have any questions we will be in contact." Maya's words slipped quietly from her lips. She closed her eyes and exhaled as she stood to her feet.

"Maya, wait, we have a bit more to do." Mr. Sloan stood to his feet and grabbed an iPad from a nearby table. Maya dropped back into her chair apprehensively.

What more could there be? Maya watched as the attorney flipped open the iPad and tapped the screen. She cut her eyes towards Jeniva. Jeniva's knuckles were gripped to the arms of the chair.

"Breathe," Maya whispered tenderly to her sister. She could

see the angst build within her. Jeniva exhaled slowly and turned her attention towards the iPad.

"Your parents had some things they personally wanted to tell you. In the event of their untimely deaths, they recorded a message." Mr. Sloan said.

A surge of adrenaline coursed through Maya's body. She jolted upright in her seat and stared intently at the dark screen. The thought of hearing her parents' voice one last time made her heart feel as if it was going to explode in her chest. The chaotic rhythm of her breath escaped her lips as she struggled to breathe.

He tapped the screen and their mom and dad's faces popped into view. Maya's eyes welled with tears as she dropped her head and closed her eyes. Jeniva, enthralled by the visions of her parents, leaned forward and softly caressed the screen. She longed to touch them one last time.

"Are you ladies ready?" Mr. Sloan spoke.

"Yes."

He pressed the play button and their parent's image came alive. The video was older, they were youthful and happy. No words had been spoken yet, they were seated gazing at one another smiling. Her mother's lips spread across her face. Her eyes glistened with just a tinge of sadness. Maya looked at Jeniva again, taking in her features. From her tightly coiled curls and her latte colored skin, Jeniva was the spitting image of their mother. She had always known it but seeing her mother's youthful face mirror the same expressions as Jeniva made it was undeniable. Her parents were so beautiful to her, and she had spent countless days searching for pieces of them within her own features.

"If you are watching this," the sound of her father's deep baritone voice captured her attention and she turned again towards the iPad. His ebony skin glistening from an unseen light source in the video, "Then, unfortunately, we are both no longer with you. I am so sorry my beautiful daughters that we have left you, but always know you are not alone, you carry our love and lessons in your heart always." Her father's voice trailed off as he looked towards their mother. Her curly auburn hair fell carelessly in her face as she leaned her head against their father's shoulder before speaking.

"Jeniva," her voice was soft, "my beautiful angel know that you are always loved. Even though we are not here with you, be strong, and live your life. I know you sweet daughter, please don't let our death be the death of you." She paused for a moment before continuing. Maya's heartbeat quickened. She wondered what her mother's last and parting words would be for her. What would the woman she always depended on leave her with to move forward in her life? At the moment, Maya felt as if she wasn't going to be able to make it without them, but she also knew that she had to.

"Maya. We have known since the moment you entered our lives that you were special. From your cappuccino colored creamy skin to your raven curls and stormy gray eyes, you have always been a sight and we loved you from the moment we laid eyes on you." Her mother paused and looked towards her father. Maya could tell from the back and forth glances of her parents that there was a secret between them. Their shifty eyes and pursing lips said what their mouths were not.

Had they kept a secret from her all of these years? Her thoughts were erratic as she wondered what it was. Her father continued where her mother left off.

"Maya always know that we chose you, and we had every intention of telling you this, but with each passing year, it got harder and harder. We don't have many answers to the time before we entered your life but we knew from the moment we laid eyes on you, you were ours. So we adopted you and raised you as our own, loved you as if Grace had birthed you herself." They fell silent for a moment.

"Adopted?" Maya spoke aloud as she looked from the video to her sister to the lawyer for answers. Tears poured from her eyes as the earth shattering realization that her parents, Grace and Anthony, were not her parents, and they had chosen to lie to her all of her life.

"I know this is hard to understand, and I wish we were there to explain it to you, there is still a lot we do not understand. We have left in a safety deposit box all that we know. It's your right to know where you come from but always know that we are your parents and we love you." The video ended, freezing their faces before the screen went black.

Maya was devastated by the news. Her body was motionless as her mind raced. She was struggling to process the facts she had been given. She was at a loss for words. The attorney watched as the two both sat in silence. This video and two more with them recorded separately had been left in his care with instructions. He recalled the paranoia that sometimes seemed to surround Anthony and Grace but he never fully understood it. Refocusing his attention on the present, Attorney Sloan stood and walked towards her with a locked box.

"Here are the contents of the safety deposit box your parents left in my care. This includes everything they knew about your past. If there is anything I can do, just let me know." He handed her the box.

The long rectangular box felt cold and heavy in her grasp. Maya's body became heated as a volt of electricity flew through her. She attempted to stand but her body became limp as her vision blurred, before going black. Maya's body hit the floor with a thud as she dreamed of a baby, a small baby in a circle of salt, surrounded by black smoke.

Chapter Three

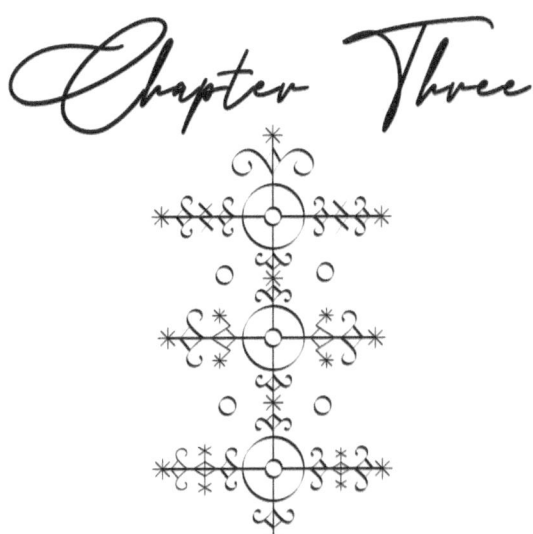

The rain-drenched the city of Seattle as Maya stared blankly out the window. In a matter of a few days, her life had been completely turned upside down and the weight of her newfound information paralyzed her. Tiny pools of tears gathered in the corners of her eyes. Her heart ached at the loss of her parents and her new found information. It felt as if life was slowly squeezing the light from her soul, slowly leaving a void where her identity used to be. The tears slid from her eyes, gradually releasing bits of her sorrow.

"How can everything be so confusing but make so much sense?" Maya spoke but there was no one there to answer. She sat alone at the kitchen table wondering how she would move forward. She loved her sister but Maya needed this time alone. She desperately wanted to process the information without having to wear a mask to calm her sister.

Her eyes strayed from the dismal rain and landed on the metal box she had been given. It was a rectangular shaped box with a small lock on it. The key was already inserted, she just needed to turn it slightly to open and reveal its contents. Maya touched the box, the metal felt cold beneath her skin. As she held it her heartbeat quickened, increasing swiftly as she persuaded herself to open it. Maya knew once she opened the box her world would forever be changed. The longer she procrastinated, the longer time stood still, and she didn't have to move forward in her new knowledge of being adopted. Maya knew that her sister wanted to be here when she opened this box, but Jeniva was gone to the store and even though there were no secrets between her sister and her, this was something she felt she had to do on her own.

Maya twisted the key slowly until she heard the small click that signaled it had been unlocked. With one hand on each side of the box, she lifted it slowly. The top felt like it was weighted with bricks as she pushed it back, exposing the contents of the box. She released a heavy sigh and reached inside the box. Her fingers rubbed against the fragile paper. It felt soft and slightly fuzzy in her hands. The paper was worn and yellowed with age. Maya could tell it had been tucked away in the box for many, many years. On the very top was a birth certificate. Maya's eyes roamed the faded bluish paper.

"State of Louisiana, Certification of Vital Record." Saying the words aloud made it even more real for her. Pieces of her slowly chipped away as she read the document. All the things she had known about herself were crumbling. Everything she thought she knew was fading swiftly.

Louisiana. The word kept replaying in her mind. All she had ever known was the West Coast, Washington State, Louisiana seemed worlds away. Maya exhaled attempting to release the despair and tension she felt in the pit of her stomach, but the release of breath did little to calm her. The more she stared at the birth certificate the more certain she was that her life had been a lie.

Her hand slipped back within her box of secrets and

grasped a newspaper article. She stared at the yellowed paper, wondering how in the world it connected to who she was.

"The Times-Picayune," Maya said again to no one. Her eyes scanned the clipping. The date on the paper was November 1, 1994, one day after her birthday. Maya briefly wondered why her parents felt this piece of paper was so important to who she was. Her eyes roamed the headline.

"Baby found in cemetery," Maya read the headline aloud. Her fingers trembled as she held the paper, her eyes locked to the headline. She read.

By Iris Bissett

A tragic scene was found in the St. Louis **Cemetery** No. 1, in Orleans Parish, Friday, October 31. The Halloween scene was straight out of a Hollywood horror movie. A small child thought to be only a few hours old was found near a deceased woman. The woman has not yet been identified.

From the salt circle formed in the middle of the cemetery, authorities believe the woman performed a ritualistic form of voodoo or hoodoo, before killing herself. Witnesses say they indeed saw a woman running through the streets barefoot before entering into the graveyard. Alarmed by her frantic demeanor police were called but were not able to make it on the scene before the macabre scene played out. Authorities have yet to release any further information about the child or the woman she was found lying next to. New Orleans Police are working to identify the abandoned baby found in an attempt to make sense of the chilling occurrence.

Maya's hands shook as she held the fragile paper in her grasp. Her brain raced in an attempt to make sense of what she had just read. The picture next to the article was a morbid scene of a cemetery. There was no baby in the picture but the mausoleums and salt circle were still in full display. Her heart raced. Staring at the scene shook her to her core. This had been her introduction to the world, a morbid scene in an old cemetery in New Orleans, Louisiana. Maya closed her eyes, "It doesn't get any weirder than this."

Why did my parents keep this? What relevance could it possibly have to me? Maya glanced back at the birth certificate as her mind connected the dots. Tears flooded her eyes as she realized she must have been the baby in the cemetery.

"What the hell?" Maya shouted out in the empty room as she stood, backing away from the table and toppling over the contents of her mystery box. The papers flew in the air. The only other thing inside the box was a picture. Maya watched as the photograph wafted in the air and landed on the hard tiled floor. She looked down at the picture. It was a picture of a woman. Her eyes were the first thing she noticed. It was like looking at a photo of herself. The woman's hair was as black as night, just like Maya's hair. Her skin, a lightly toasted brown that closely resembled her own. But the biggest resemblance she saw was her eyes. The dewy gray pools were deep and haunting. The woman's eyes stared brightly back at her, almost as if she were looking directly at her. Maya bent down to pick up the picture. As soon as she touched it a wave of heat rushed over her body.

Maya, I did it for you. I love you more than life.

A whispered voice floated through the empty house. Maya turned from side to side, looking over her shoulder in search of the voice that called out to her. Her eyes again landed on the photograph in her hands. The woman appeared to move as she mouthed inaudible words. *Maya, Maya, can you hear me?* The whispers shot through the house again while Maya watched the woman in the picture continue her ghostly movement to communicate with her.

"What the hell is happening to me?" Maya again asked herself questions she didn't know the answers to. Maya tossed the picture as she began to shake. She had no control over what was happening to her. Waves of heat scorched her body from head to toe. Her limbs went limp and her body numb as the heat intensified. Maya's eyes fluttered as she tried to focus on her surroundings. The lightheaded dizziness caused her to stumble as she tried to make her way back to her seat at the kitchen table. She gripped the chair and stood for a moment. Maya closed her eyes, seeing the woman's vibrant gaze and beautiful face, right before succumbing to nothingness. Her body landed on the hard floor as everything faded to black.

Chapter Four

"Maya!" Jeniva shouted as she entered the kitchen, finding Maya laying motionless. The sight of her sister lying lifeless against the floor petrified her. Jeniva raced to Maya's unconscious body and slid to her side. She softly pulled Maya's head into her lap and hugged her tightly. She grasped Maya's hands and shook her attempting to wake her. Jeniva's breaths were short as she struggled to fight the uncontrolled anxiety that was building within her. Her hands shook as she tightened her grip on Maya's hand, "Maya wake up, I can't lose you too, Maya!" She shouted again.

Maya's body laid unresponsive. Jeniva laid her back down against the tile and listened for her breath. Numerous thoughts dashed through her mind. She knew she would never recover if she lost Maya too. Once she realized Maya was still breathing she exhaled a sigh of relief. With the anxiety somewhat dissipating, Jeniva steadied herself and tried again to wake her sister.

"Maya!" She shouted again. She stared down at Maya,

contemplating how long she should wait before calling 911. Just as she was about to reach for her phone, Maya began to move. "Thank God!" Maya rubbed her head as she tried to sit up. A bit dizzy, she slowly stood to her feet.

"What's wrong, we need to get you to the doctor," Jeniva's eyes glazed over with concern. She had already lost both of her parents, the thought of losing the only other person she had in this world terrified her and she felt compelled to stop anything else horrible from happening.

"I'm ok." Maya weakly smiled and hugged Jeniva. She could see the terror in her eyes and she didn't want her to worry about her.

"No, you're not. How long have you been having these fainting spells? This is the second one that I know of and people don't just start passing out for no reason. You need to see a doctor, we need to make sure this isn't something serious," Jeniva's voice raised.

She knew Maya was going to try to act like it was nothing but she wasn't stupid, there was obviously something going on. Maya ignored her sister as she reached to pick up the scattered papers. Jeniva, irritated that her sister was ignoring her, reached and snatched the paper from Maya's hands. She tore the fragile paper from her sister's hold and poured all of her attention into it, wanting to know why it was so important to Mya that she would rather focus on this than listen to her.

"What's all this?" Jeniva flipped through the papers rapidly scanning over them.

"I, I, I really don't know Niva." Maya's voice trembled as she spoke as her eyes widened. She stared at Jeniva trying to respond but the words wouldn't flow, they were trapped in the back of her throat, held prisoner by her fear. She feared facing her unknown origins. Maya was physically and mentally exhausted. She had no idea what any of this really meant. It was all too much for her to handle. Jeniva finished reading over the article.

"So, you're obviously the baby in this article," Jeniva waved the paper back and forth in the air in front of Maya. "this is some crazy shit!" She shifted her weight from left to right as she looked down at the paper and then back to Maya. She was floored by what she was reading. "This is gruesome, no wonder mom and dad wanted to keep this buried." The mention of their parents' lie made Maya uncomfortable. She had yet to process her feelings regarding her parent's deception.

"I know." Maya weakly walked over to the table and began to put the papers back into the lockbox. She moved hurriedly, the faster she could rid herself of these papers, she could go on with her life and pretend as if none of this existed. She was desperate to put her life as close to normal as she possibly could.

"Is that all you got to say?"

"What else is there to say Jeniva?" Maya snapped at her sister.

"So you're really going to tell me that you don't want to know more about where you come from?" Jeniva crossed her arms, her eyebrows dipped and her nose crinkled as she glared at Maya.

"I come from the same place you do," Maya answered sarcastically. Her arms shot forward, desperately wanting Jeniva to see her side of things. She felt as if the rug had been completely pulled from under her and she couldn't comprehend how knowing more about this morbid history of hers could possibly be a good thing. By the tone in Maya's voice, Jeniva could tell she had pushed her sister too far. She softened her voice before continuing.

"I know you do, and I promise you, sis, that birth certificate in there doesn't make you any less my sister, or any less Grace and Anthony's child. They raised you and you are who you are because of them. But obviously Maya, they kept these things for a reason. Even though it's your past, it's your beginning and you deserve to know how things began for you." Jeniva walked over and hugged her sister. She couldn't begin to imagine how she felt, but she knew that whatever it was she would help her see it through.

Maya stood in silence as she thought of everything that Jeniva had just said. If she were being completely honest with herself she wanted to know more, but there was a side of her that didn't. So many weird things had been happening to her, she wanted to just put everything behind her.

"Maya," Jeniva said, this time her voice coated in compassion.

"I hear you but maybe I should just leave all this alone. These people that I was born to, they are obviously batshit crazy," Maya looked down at her baby sister.

"Maybe they were, at least one of them was," Jeniva nudged her sister and chuckled, "but either way I got your back. Our parents wanted you to know the truth, so go find the truth, Maya." Maya and Jeniva locked eyes, one sister hesitant, the other pleading. Jeniva's head tilted to the side, silently making her request known.

"I wouldn't know the first place to start," Maya finally broke the silence between them. She was looking for any excuse not to do this because she was deathly afraid of what she would find.

"Well, lucky for you, I did my internship as a research assistant for the Seattle Times. I got you," Jeniva dashed into the other room and then quickly returned with her MacBook in hand. "Come here." She motioned to the chair next to her as she took a seat. Maya reluctantly sat next to her sister. She wasn't sure of how much she really wanted to know, but her sister said one thing that had gotten through to her. Her parents had left these things for her, had entrusted the lawyer to make sure she received them. They could have taken this secret to the grave and she would have never known. If they went through all of this trouble to make her past known, she could at least take these first steps to learn what they wanted her to know.

"Okay, see this article was written by a woman named Iris, let's see if we can find her. She has to know something about the case since she covered it, hopefully, she can point us in the right direction." Maya could hear the excitement in Jeniva's voice as she spoke. Her fingers tapped away on the keyboard as Maya silently watched.

"So what is it that you think she could tell us?" Maya asked unsure if this was even going to work. It was almost a twenty-four year old article, Maya reasoned if they could find this woman, it was unlikely that she would be able to share any information with them.

"I think she can tell us a lot. I just need to track her down. Nine times out of ten she's still writing if she is still alive." Jeniva read over the screen as she clicked and scrolled through page after page. Her fingers moved rapidly as the zeal of a new mystery to solve coursed through her.

"I knew we could find her. Look," she pointed to the screen. Maya leaned over to see what Jeniva was pointing at, "She is no longer at the paper, but she runs a magazine called *Enchanted*, there is even a link to connect with the editor. I will send her an email and hopefully, she answers back."

Maya sank into her chair and watched her sister get lost in her research. For Jeniva it was pure excitement. It was a journey that she was happy to help her sister with, but for Maya, it was paralyzing terror that increased with every keystroke.

Chapter Five

*M*aya stirred her coffee as she stared out the window. The house was quiet as she watched the sunrise. Maya hoped that the quiet stillness of nature would calm her, but the dull ache in her heart refused to subside. From losing her parents to finding out they were not her biological parents and learning the disturbing circumstances in which she was adopted, Maya was left feeling broken and confused.

She watched as the fall wind blew the orange, red and yellow leaves, scattering them throughout the thick green grass. The dense fog that laid over the sky almost seemed as if it touched the ground. The fog swirled in the wind seeming to move closer and closer to the window. The air seemed dense but it moved fast as it twisted and turned like a tornado. Maya squinted her eyes and stared at the formation of air.

"What the hell is that?" Maya spoke aloud. She watched as the fog swayed back and forth, tumbling and tossing in the air until a form started to take shape. Maya stared as a man's face appeared in the heavy air, slowly becoming clearer and clearer. She could make out the shape of his almond eyes and the strong structured jawline. The face floated just outside the window. Maya's feet were planted in place, she was unable to move. Her pulse quickened as she closed her eyes. She shut them tight hoping her mind was playing tricks on her.

"None of this can be real! None of this can really be happening." Maya's eyes were shut so tight, little droplets had begun to line her lids. Her breaths were chaotic as she struggled to reign in her spiraling grasp on reality.

"Maya? Who are you talking to?" The sound of Jeniva's voice jolted Maya back to reality.

I have to be losing my mind! Maya opened her eyes, staring out the window. The floating face she had just seen was long gone. Maya clenched her fist at her side and counted backward from ten.

"No one, good morning," Maya said while blinking her eyes, trying to rid herself of the tears that threatened to roll down her cheeks. She released a long breath before turning to face her baby sister. *I gotta get my shit together.*

"Maya, you were clearly talking to someone. You've been doing that a lot lately. What's going on with you?" Jeniva was a little unsettled by the changes her sister was going through. She was so used to her being the rock, she didn't know how to help her slowly crumbling sister.

Both of them stood in silence. Jeniva still worried about the changes her sister was going through, but she knew she would help her at all costs. *All people have a breaking point.* Jeniva reasoned.

"Guess what!" Jeniva decided to break the uncomfortable silence that had settled between them. Persuading Maya to move forward had proved to be a difficult task for Jeniva, but she was optimistic.

"What?" Maya answered, not really in the mood for any of

Jeniva's juvenile guessing games. Jeniva's lip curled as she bit her bottom lip. Deciding to ignore her sister's attitude, she walked over to the sink and stood next to her. Holding her iPad so both of them could see it.

"I got a response from Iris Bisset." Jeniva's fingers went to work, tapping and pinching to zoom the screen.

Maya looked at Jeniva in surprise. She had humored Jeniva last night, but she never expected a reply. Receiving a reply from this woman made the contents of that box all too real to her. Anytime the topic of her past came up it made her uncomfortable, but Jeniva's excitement was undeniable and she didn't want to extinguish any of her newfound fire. Things had been so hard for the two of them, if this somehow gave Jeniva a project or a means to heal, Maya would push through. Jeniva began to read the email.

"Ms. St. James, this is a topic that I swore I would never speak on, but the details that you have mentioned in your email gives me reason to believe you may somehow be connected. I will speak with you, but not through email, text, or phone. I will only speak in person, under my home's protection," Jeniva finished. Both Maya and Jeniva thought the email was short and abrupt.

"Okay, she must be nuts," Maya smiled and moved towards her Keurig to make another cup of coffee.

"Maybe a little cryptic but you really think she's nuts?"

"I think she's a lot of nuts," Maya laughed.

"Maybe we should go?" Jeniva loved a good mystery and even though she sympathized with her sister, she felt a rush she hadn't felt since she got the news about her parents. "I think it could do both of us some good."

"How can any of this be good Jeniva?" Maya wanted to play along, but the thought of getting on a plane going clear across the country to an unfamiliar place terrified her. "Why would I want to get on an airplane fly clear across the country to meet some crazy lady that may or may not be able to help," Maya grabbed her cup and sat down at the kitchen table. She sipped slowly knowing the conversation wasn't over.

"I believe she knows something," Jeniva flopped in the chair across from Maya. "Look at it like this, this was probably the greatest and craziest story of her time, you don't ever forget a thing like that. Ever. I'm telling you this lady knows something because if this were my story I wouldn't let go until my questions were answered." Maya shook her head as Jeniva talked.

"You're not going to let this go, are you?" Maya's eyebrows dipped as she pressed her lips into a straight line. She knew her sister and she understood that she wouldn't let this go until she got her way.

"No."

"Well, I have work and you have school." Maya shot back, she was looking for any reason to get out of what her sister was proposing. She was terrified of what she could possibly find if she decided to embark on this journey. She didn't know what sordid details would be revealed and Maya didn't believe her heart could stand anymore heartache.

"Everything is submitted online, I can do it literally anywhere, and as for the hospital, they need to find another social worker for now. What you do is important and sis, you're amazing at it but right now you have to put you first, don't you want to know something?" Jeniva reasoned with Maya but Maya was exhausted from the verbal jousting that was taking place. "annnnnnnnd we can make it a birthday turnup!" Jeniva reached out and touched her sister's hand, hoping she was getting through to her. She knew changing her sister's mind was no easy task, and she was willing to try any tool in her toolbox.

"Turn up huh? I do not turn up!" Maya rolled her eyes at the thought of partying in the crowded streets of New Orleans. Jeniva immediately saw the look on Maya's face.

"Maybe it's what we both need though Maya, a break from all the grief." Jeniva's lips slowly spread into a smile. Maya wasn't sure there wouldn't be more grief waiting for her in New Orleans, but if this meant that much to her sister she would do it. Tragedy had almost broken them both, and Maya felt if she could give a small bit of happiness to her sister then she would do so.

"Okay fine, I guess I will make the arrangements, " Maya conceded.

Jeniva waved her hands in the air, stopping Maya mid-sentence. "I got it, I will plan everything just get your time off from work and I will handle the rest. I'm thinking we will leave Friday!"

Jeniva jumped up from the chair, hugging her sister tightly before she left the room. She understood her sister's hesitation, but she thought it would be good for her. And no matter what they found, Jeniva knew she would stand by her sister's side, come heaven or hell.

Chapter Six

The humid southern weather hit Maya as soon as she exited the plane. For the end of October, it felt unusually hot to her. Compared to the mild comfort of her west coast home, New Orleans felt like a sauna. Maya and Jeniva watched as the rental car was being driven to them. She looked at Jeniva, a look of intrigue and excitement washed over Jeniva's face as she stared back at Maya. She was so excited she could hardly contain her excitement. Maya, however, felt differently. She wasn't ready to leap into this mystery head first.

"Do you mind if I get some rest when we get to the hotel?" Maya asked. She knew her sister was ready to explore, but she didn't have the energy or interest at the moment. Maya was flooded with anxiety and apprehension and it was exhausting.

"Sure, I'll just go grab us something to eat, while you rest." Jeniva smiled as they loaded their bags and then slid in the car. She was a bit disappointed but she also understood she needed to allow Maya to move at a slower pace. Jeniva could tell this was difficult for her sister, so she decided she would continue to push, but would do it gently.

The ride from the airport to her hotel was short. They looked out the window, both in awe of the vibrancy and mystique New Orleans seemed to hold. They had never been further than Las Vegas, and they could immediately see the South held a charm and old world feel that they had never before experienced.

Both women took in the sights and sounds. Maya could feel the excitement that rested over the city. It's as if the air was alive, buzzing with electricity and unadulterated jubilation. It felt different to Maya. She shifted in her seat, unaware of why she felt so frenzied since landing.

Maybe it's because we are meeting this lady tonight. Maya thought to herself as she got out of her car and loaded the luggage cart with her things. The last few weeks had crippled her with fatigue. After checking in, a bellhop rolled a gold luggage cart to them and transferred their luggage before heading towards the elevator.

"This hotel is beautiful," Maya looked around the opulent hotel. Its beauty could not be denied and somehow to Maya, it seemed old and modern all at the same time.

"I know, I chose it because it's nice and spooky, it's supposedly haunted." A slow smile spread across Jeniva's face. With her sister's birthday being on Halloween, she wanted to give her an experience she would never forget.

The bellhop looked at both of them before rolling the cart onto the elevator, "It is haunted ladies." He stood tall and slim, his dark skin glowing as the dim lights flickered before the elevator doors closed.

"I don't believe in that," Maya responded, dismissing his comments.

"It's not about what you believe, it's about what simply is," his tone was low, his voice barely above a whisper. "Pay close attention, you will see doors opening and closing by themselves, guests have seen Red, an employee who died here and has continued to roam the halls of the hotel during his afterlife. And sometimes you will hear the laughter of a toddler ringing through the halls of the hotel. Don't be scared though, it's just the friendly ghost of Maurice. In the 1800s, his parents left him in the care of a nanny for a night out. The young boy developed a fever and died in his room, now his spirit is earthbound, destined to play in the halls and rooms of the Monteleone Hotel for eternity." He again smiled, exposing his stark white teeth, and then winked at the women.

"Okay, that's enough," Jeniva could tell Maya was getting a little spooked. They finished the short walk to their suite, she tipped him and abruptly shut the door. "All right, I'm gonna head back out to find us something to eat, I'll be back and then after we eat, we can head over to see Iris Bissett." Jeniva smiled. *Damn, she low-key looks like she's losing her mind.*

"What?" Maya looked at Jeniva.

"I said I'm going to get something to eat."

"I know, after that, you said I'm losing my mind."

"What are you talking about, no one said you were." Jeniva was certain she hadn't said that aloud. She shook her head from side to side as her brow furrowed. She didn't plan on going down this road with Maya. Again. "I'll be back." She said through an exasperated breath. Jeniva paused as she stood outside the door, gathering her thoughts. She looked back at the door one last time, worried about her sister. *She will be okay, once we know something, she will be okay.* Jeniva reasoned with herself as she walked away.

Back inside the room, Maya fell onto the bed and curled her body as she held on to herself. Tears threatened to burst through. She questioned her sanity. Maya hadn't confirmed anything to her sister, but she knew she was hearing things. She was starting to see and feel things that didn't make sense.

As the tears rolled down her eyes she wished now more than ever that her parents were still here, at least they could comfort her as they had always done.

"Am I losing my mind?" No one answered as she adjusted her head against the pillow and closed her eyes. If she could just get a few moments of sleep maybe it would reaffirm that she wasn't losing her grasp on reality. Maya's eyelids fluttered as she slipped into a desperately needed slumber.

"Maya," His voice was like the soothing sounds of a saxophone playing a song only she could hear. She turned and looked towards the direction that the voice called from. Standing outside she could smell the salty ocean water as the waves crashed against the beach. The sandy coastline slid between her toes as she searched for the person uttering such sweet sounds.

Her breaths shortened as he approached. His chocolate skin seemed to glow in the iridescent light of the moon as he emerged from the briny water. Droplets of liquid dripped from his skin as he approached. His dark brown eyes seemed to catch the light and sparkle as she stood frozen. Maya looked at the man, not knowing and knowing him all at the same time.

Electric currents pulsed through her body as he moved closer, every nerve ending was on fire. The closer he got the clearer he became. His body was completely bare and his frame was tall and muscular as if someone had melted dark chocolate and poured it over his sculpted physique.

"I've been waiting for you." He spoke.

"For me?" Maya asked.

"Yes, for you to come back."

"Come back?" She questioned.

A smile spread across his face exposing perfectly white teeth. He caressed the side of her face with his palms as he slid his hands behind her head and pulled her into him. His lips pressed against hers, his tongue slowly probing until he gained entrance between her lips. Instinctively, her arms slid around his neck, holding tightly to him and the pleasure his kisses brought. His hands softly traveled down her bare spine, lightly tapping her skin with his fingertips.

She moaned softly as her head dropped backward. His tongue explored her body. She opened her eyes staring at the man.

"*Who are you?" Maya asked.*

"*I am yours,"*

The man laid her against the sandy beach, still kissing her body. She surrendered to his every command. His body rubbed against hers, causing a fire to stir below. She pushed her body as close to him as she could get. Her back arched as he planted kisses along her neck. Her desire to feel him was overwhelming.

"Maya!" The sound of Jeniva's voice jolted her awake. She groggily rose from the bed struggling to open her eyes and focus on Jeniva.

"Yeah," She mumbled.

"You okay, sounded like you were having a bad dream," Jeniva handed her a styrofoam plate of food and a plastic fork. Maya took the food and had a seat at the small table in the room.

"I don't know, what time are we supposed to meet with her," Maya asked, desperate to change the conversation and the thoughts of the man invading her head.

Chapter Seven

"I don't know about this Jeniva," Maya wished that she hadn't agreed to any of it, but quickly reminded herself of the excitement her sister displayed every time she spoke about it.

"It doesn't matter now, it's too late we are already here," Jeniva steered the car down the long dirt road. The pair had no idea where they were. It seemed as if it had taken forever to reach the destination. The car rolled to a stop in front of a two-story white, plantation-style home with massive columns and a large mossy tree dangling in front of the evenly spaced windows.

"You ready?" Jeniva asked while opening the door and stepping out of the car. Maya sat frozen inside, paralyzed by the fear of what she would find out about her. Everything that she knew of her birth was some sorted tale that someone would see in a horror movie, not anything that happened in real life. Yet somehow, it was happening to her.

"Get out of the car!" Jeniva tapped on the passenger side window and then held her hands out with her palms up. "Get out, it's too late to back out!" Maya looked towards her sister and reluctantly opened the door.

"Let's get this over with. I really don't think she will have much to tell us. What could she possibly know that she didn't put in that article?" Maya asked.

"A lot, that was only one article that our parents clipped, just keep an open mind, Maya. Maybe she knows something, maybe she doesn't but it's one step closer to knowing something more than you did yesterday."

The gravel driveway crunched under their feet as the pair walked towards the front door. As they approached they both noticed the red dusty substance that seemed to surround the house.

"What's this?" Jeniva reached down and ran her finger through the chalky powder on the ground.

"I don't know, but should you really be touching it?" Maya squinted as she watched Jeniva run her fingers through the dirt. The creaking door caught their attention as it swung open.

"Leave that alone child!" The small woman exited the house and quickly recovered the newly formed break in her red dust. "You ought not go touching things you don't understand," She finished.

"We're sorry," Maya spoke up, apologizing for her sister's forward actions. "Are you Ms. Bissett?"

"Yes, and you are?"

"I'm Maya and this is my sister Jeniva," Maya said pointing towards her sister. "We emailed you about an article we found."

Iris looked at Jeniva and then back towards Maya. She could tell from the moment she laid eyes on her who she was. She sensed her presence far before she saw her and when she finally opened the door, she knew exactly who she was.

"Come in," She said as she opened the front door and watched the two walk into her house. The small-framed woman walked slowly as her long auburn hair swung from side to side with each step, her golden bronzed skin catching glimmers of the candlelight that blazed a trail throughout the house. She led them to a dining room.

"Have a seat," she motioned towards the available chairs and they both took a seat at the table. Iris walked to a desk and opened it pulling out a shoebox filled with papers tumbling from it. She placed it on the table and sat across from Maya and Jeniva.

"I apologize for touching the stuff around the door. I was just curious about what it was," Jeniva dusted the remaining of the red substance from her hands as she spoke.

"Curious huh, if you're curious then ask a question," Iris paused and looked up from her papers, "you don't go around touching and messing stuff you don't understand. That outside this house is red brick dust. I have it all around the property. No one that means me harm can pass it." Iris eyed both of the women. The petite one to her seemed pushy and overbearing, and Iris did not like that. She closed her eyes and exhaled, deciding not to judge the young lady on her eager ways. She had agreed to help her with information in her email and Iris Bisset always kept her word.

She slowly began to layout clippings of articles and handwritten notes on the table. After she removed all of the contents from the box she stood again and walked back to the desk. Both Maya and Jeniva watched in silence, neither of them knowing what or why she was doing what she was doing.

Iris returned to the table and pulled out a white candle, a large twine-wrapped bunch of leaves, and a glass bowl. Maya's heartbeat quickened as she watched the strange woman pull out more odd items. Iris was quiet as she worked her way through her home, retrieving all of the items she felt she needed. Maya looked at Jeniva with raised eyebrows as they watched her light one of the bundles of leaves and began to wave it in the air. She walked backward as she swept the smokey substance from left to right until she made it to her front door. She opened the door for a moment and continued.

"What the hell is she doing?" Maya leaned forward attempting to see the front of the house. "I think we need to go, all this craziness makes me uneasy." Maya leaned into Jeniva, staring her straight in the eye.

"Relax, Maya. We knew she was a little bit on the looney side because she wouldn't just answer the email. Humor her for a moment, she might actually know some things." Jeniva glanced over at the paper Iris had laid out. It appeared to be clippings much like the one her parents had left for Maya. Jeniva desperately wanted to touch it, but Iris had become unraveled when she touched her brick dust, she didn't want to be lectured again, so she patiently waited for her to return and get started.

"So how much longer is she going to be doing this weird shit. We just need to know what she knows and we can go." Maya blew a breath out.

"Everything is revealed in its own time." Jeniva and Maya turned towards the sound of the voice, startled by his sudden presence.

"Oh shit, you scared the hell out of me." She looked towards the man standing in the doorway. "How long have you been standing there?"

"Long enough to know how impatient you both are. Relax, everything she's doing is for protection." He smiled and took a seat. Maya looked him over without saying a word. He had the same creamy golden hued skin and wavy red hair that Iris had.

"Protection from what?" Maya asked, her voice cracked as she spoke.

"From the same thing your mother was running from that night." Iris re-entered the room and stood across from them.

"Eau, s'il vous plaît" Iris spoke to the man, passing him the empty glass bowl."He is going to put water into the bowl and then we will get started."

She sat down again across from them and opened a bottle and began to pour it over her hands. The scent floated in the air as she worked the liquid over her hands and between her fingers. The man returned and placed the bowl of water in the center of the table. Iris then struck a match and lit the candle that had been placed on the table. Maya stared at her. Iris's actions were making her uneasy. Her skin prickled with tiny piercing needles, giving her chills that ran the length of her spine to her neck. Heat washed over Maya as she watched the woman rock back and forth and chant some unrecognizable song.

Maya swallowed the lump that was forming in her throat. Iris stood and grabbed a white chalky substance, mixed it with her fragrant water, and created a pasty substance. She took two fingers and circled it in the pasty substance and then rubbed it at the base of her neck and spine.

"What is all this?" Jeniva questioned, "This is starting to look like a scene from *The Skeleton Key* and that is not what we signed up for. We came to talk, that's it." Although she was eager to find out what the once reporter knew, she didn't like the way this was going. Even though she had just tried to calm her sister's anxiety, this was starting to be too much. Iris continued, ignoring Jeniva's comment. As she rocked back and forth the lights in the room began to flicker, causing shadows to bounce off of the wall. A cold chill flew through the air, even though there were no open windows or fans to cause it. The open door to the room slammed shut.

"The Skeleton Key was just a movie, this is real life," She paused for a moment as the man handed her a deck of cards, and then he took a seat beside her. "this is for protection. You will come to understand that what you see in this world is only surface deep. The Cascarilla and Florida water will give us clarity and protection, and I've seen what's coming your way Maya, you're going to need it."

The chill in her voice frosted the air with angst and alarm. Maya reached under the table they sat at and held Jeniva's hand.

Jeniva leaned over and whispered into Maya's ear, "What the fuck have I gotten us into?"

Chapter Eight

*J*eniva rested her back against the chair as she held Maya's hand tightly. The woman that sat across from her was not what she pictured. To her, Iris Bissett was supposed to be an untapped wealth of knowledge. But instead, Jeniva saw a woman who was unraveling fast.

"So what is this, Voodoo or something?" Jeniva couldn't control the words that flowed from her mouth. Iris smiled at the pushy one's questions.

"Voodoo is a religion. This is a mix of many things and goes by many names. Voodoo, Hoodoo, Santeria, folk magick, witchcraft, depends on where you are from but religion is only half of what I'm doing. This is for protection." Iris said.

"You keep saying that. Protection from what?" Jeniva was becoming annoyed and starting to think that maybe her sister was right. Maybe Iris was some lady that was once a reporter that did a story and that was it.

"Your mother," Iris faced Maya, ignoring the other's question. This wasn't about her, "was from a long line of natural witches, voodoo priestess who practiced the religion of Voodoo, which slowly evolved, it wasn't just a religion it was the practice of native and African spiritualism, hoodoo, and some would even say it was witchcraft." Jeniva and Maya slowly turned to face one another. Jeniva was starting to rethink her position on coming here. It was clear that this woman had somehow lost her mind.

"I think it's time to go," Jeniva spoke. She reached for Maya's sleeve, gently tugging to pull her away from the table. What was happening was getting too weird, she feared she had walked into some type of hustle and was pretty sure this woman would start asking for money to remove some fake hex, and Jeniva had no intention of allowing this woman to play on her sister's emotions.

Maya's eyes widened in an attempt to calm her sister. After being here, her position on what this woman may or may not know began to shift. It was obvious from the article her mother really was connected to this occult world, and even though she knew it sounded insane, this was the only person she knew that had some type of connection to her biological family. Crazy or not, Maya was going to hear her out. Seeing her sister didn't plan to move, Jeniva fell back into her seat, closely keeping an eye on Iris.

"What can you tell me about this?" At the mention of Maya's biological family, she became inquisitive. Jeniva had convinced her to come, but now that Maya was here she was determined to see it through. It's as if she was supposed to be in this moment, she couldn't understand it but she could feel it.

She released Jeniva's grasp and went into her purse and laid out the article she found. "Our parents, left me this in a lockbox when they died and my sister thought you might be able to tell me more. The article doesn't say who she was or what she was doing." Maya questioned. The more she questioned, the hotter the room became. Her heart raced as beads of sweat lined the corners of her forehead.

"Your parents' death, was no accident. I wrote this article almost twenty-five years ago. When you were found in that cemetery. This was the story that changed my life, the one that I couldn't let go of. " Iris dropped her head and bit her lip before continuing. The words were on the tip of her tongue, but a quarter century's old memories flooded her mind. She swallowed the lump she could feel forming in her throat before continuing. "The night your mother had you, she was running from a presence so evil, the only way she knew to protect you was to sacrifice herself."

"Evil? Sacrifice? What do you mean sacrifice herself?" Maya questioned.

"I mean exactly what I said, she wasn't in that cemetery by accident, she was casting one of the most powerful spells she could conjure to protect you," Iris answered.

"Wait, wait, what do you mean conjuring a spell?" Maya turned to face her sister, not needing any words to know what she was thinking. This was absolutely crazy to her.

"The paper sent me because I followed the stories that no one wanted to write, the strange occult type stories that always seemed to happen here in the Crescent City. The type of stories that no one ever wanted to talk about." Iris paused to reach for the stack of papers that she pulled out when they first walked in.

Her long boney fingers spread them out one by one in front of Maya. Maya's eyes roamed the pictures, not truly understanding what she was seeing. She could see a baby and a circle, the gates of the cemetery, and a covered body laying on the ground. It was gruesome.

"The closer and closer I got to the truth the further away from it I became."

"What does that mean?" Jeniva was tired of her riddles. The

two had been there for more than an hour and still had no more information than what they came with. Ignoring Jeniva, Iris continued.

"You're mother was running from something that night. Scared. I interviewed people who had seen her running barefoot with you, a newborn in her arms. Something was after her and the only way she knew to stop it was to cover you." Maya listened. She didn't understand much of what was being said. Being told your mother was a Voodoo queen wasn't something she was prepared to hear. Until now, thoughts of things like Hoodoo, spiritualism, and witchcraft were unknown to her. She barely knew that her zodiac sign was Scorpio, the closest she came to magick was reading her horoscope.

"What was she running from? What could scare her so much that she would kill herself and leave her baby?" Maya asked. She didn't understand what type of mother would just give up and not fight for her child. Her parents had always fought and stood for her. Maya sat back in her chair and stared at the floor, despising the idea that she was somehow connected to this woman.

"Hand me the blessed water." She lifted her eyes, at the sound of Iris's voice. Maya watched as Iris carefully poured the liquid into the glass bowl in front of her. Next, she sprinkled in what appeared to Maya to be some sort of dried flowers and herbs.

Maya and Jeniva stared as Iris's eyes closed. The candles that burned began to flicker and sway to some invisible source. Iris reached out and grabbed the man's hand.

"We are seers, my son and I. We can see the past, the present, and the future. Whatever our spirit guides want to make known to us is shown. This is how I am able to get so much more on any story I do, but with your mother I could only see so far, I tried to break the barriers and blocks around her but I could only see black. The more I tried, the more I felt the effects of the black magick that shrouded her. I lost my sight until I stopped searching. "Iris poured a tea like concoction into a cup with her free hand.

Jeniva stared at Iris, convinced she was truly crazy. She waved her hands in the air, "What the hell is really going on, look ma'am, I'm not sure what you think we came here for but this isn't it. I just wanted information so my sister could find out about her family. I didn't come here for a seance or seer!" Jeniva faced Maya, "Let's go."

Maya sat silently staring down at her feet. She felt a buzz of energy flowing through her ever since they had walked through the door. The way Iris and her son were talking it truly scared her, but some part of her needed to see it through. "No, I don't want to go, I want to know what she knows," Maya whispered while slowly lifting her eyes back to the table. She didn't bother to face her sister, she didn't want to see the disappointment that she undoubtedly had on her face.

Jeniva shifted back in her seat. She wanted to be angry with her sister, this was nuts, but she thought of all the times her sister had been there for her, the way she always protected her, almost like a second mother. Jeniva wanted to leave, but for her sister, she would stay. She reached under the table and grabbed Maya's hand again and squeezed, silently signaling that she was here with her.

"Drink this," Iris slid the liquid towards Maya.

"What is it?" Maya quizzed.

"Drink. It will open up your third eye and allow us to be psychically linked."

Maya stared at the liquid and then at Jeniva. Jeniva's eyes said don't but her lips never moved. Maya cautiously reached for the liquid and picked it up. The warm glass seemed to vibrate. She lifted the glass to her lips and allowed the heated liquid to slip past her tongue and glide down her throat.

"Your energy is strong, your mother bound your powers as

apart of her sacrifice but it was not permanent. I saw this the first time I followed the story. Let me show you."

Iris and the man reached for Maya's hand and completed the circle. As soon as their hands joined Maya was flooded with heat. Her body shook as her eyes rolled showing nothing but white and then settling in an absent gaze. Jeniva waved her hand in front of Maya but received no response. She watched in horror as all three seemed to be present but not present at all. Jeniva shook Maya but there was no response.

Maya could feel the gentle shake but the pull of the past was too strong. Her mind linked to the other two. Her thoughts were their thoughts and theirs were hers. Black smoked billowed in front of them and then she felt her mind being yanked to another time, to another place she was not familiar with.

Maya saw a woman running with a baby. She was tattered and bleeding as her bare feet hit the ground. The images flashed in and out before stopping.

"I won't let you do it!" The pregnant woman yelled at the tall man that stood before her. He towered over the small woman. The woman was the reflection of Maya. Even though small she exuded strength.

"We have to, the prophecy has to be fulfilled."

"I don't give a shit about that! This is our baby. How could you?" The tall man reached for her. Pulling her small frame into him.

"What can we do? If we don't fulfill the covenant our ancestors made at the crossroads they will never give us peace."

"I can't Antan. We can't."

"We knew what our union would cause, a baby from both of our bloodlines was the reason why we were warned to stay away from each other. But we didn't and now this is the fulfillment of a promise that neither of us made, but for the sake of the children we will have in the future and to finally have peace, we have to give her to them. Look," he gently lifted her head stroked her cheek before kissing her softly on the lips, "we will have twenty-five wonderful years with her, we will build a family and they will know love and peace because of her." The man finished.

"Antan, I can't. I can't sacrifice our daughter for the sake of anyone. Maybe we have come as far as we can. I love you. I'm willing to die to protect our daughter. What if I could conjure a spell to protect her, remove her powers?"

"How when they are always watching? Marcelle, you are powerful but not powerful enough to keep them from knowing and besides, you know you can never remove her powers. Even if they are dormant they will always be there." Antan's tone was drenched with concern. He needed her to see things his way, for everyone's safety.

She glanced at the candles burning. The spell she cast gave them cover long enough to have these conversations, giving her an idea. "I think I can protect her. I love you Antan. I love was a forbidden one. I cherish every moment we had." Just as she finished speaking a gust of wind blew through the small home, blowing out the candles. The door flew open slamming against the wall as a shadowy figure appeared at the doorway. The pair turned to face the direction of the noise.

"Get out of here Marcelle!" He screamed. Marcelle began to run as fast as her feet would carry her. The man uttered unrecognizable phrases at the shadowy figured standing at the door. A sinister smile spread across the man at the door. As he brought his hands up, making visible a small doll that resembled Antan. He snarled as he twisted the head of the doll and shoved a long black pin into the chest. Just as he did, Anton's body went limp and tumbled to the floor.

Maya screamed as her body jolted sending her tumbling back and onto the floor. Her heart raced uncontrollably as she tried to make sense of the images in her head.

"That's it, we are leaving!" Jeniva shouted. She had enough of whatever this was. She pulled Maya to her feet and dragged her to the rental car. Iris and son watched as the two exited their home.

"Christian, did you feel that?"

"Yes, I did." He replied to his mother knowing she was speaking of the immense power that already emanated from Maya.

"The unbinding isn't complete and her powers are already ten times stronger than her mother's or father. Watch her," Iris tapped the center of her forehead. "She's going to need our help."

Chapter Nine

"What the hell happened in there?" Jeniva asked as they entered the hotel room. Maya didn't say a word the entire ride back. She couldn't. Maya didn't yet know how to put into words what she had been seeing.

"I don't know."

"Well, I'm sorry I dragged you to see that batty old lady. I think we should go down to Bourbon St., have some fun and then Sunday get the hell out of here and back to Washington. You don't need this. You know who your parents were. Grace and Anthony. It doesn't matter if you were adopted. You are my sister, you are their daughter. Not these other people." After witnessing the person Iris was, the more her position flipped. Jeniva thought this would be a fun getaway to take their minds off of their parents' death, but it had somehow turned into a bad scene from a horror movie. As far as Jeniva was concerned, this was over.

Jeniva walked towards Maya and embraced her. She sensed her sister needed a hug. She thought this trip would help but it seemed that it had only hurt. Maya released Jeniva and laid against the bed. Everything that happened exhausted her. Her eyes fluttered before she fell asleep.

Jeniva watched as her sister slept. Maya's breathing was heavy as she released a troubled sigh every few seconds. Jeniva had never seen her sister so vulnerable, and what she thought would help her find closure had only ripped a cavern sized wound within her sister. If Jeniva was being completely honest with herself, she had pushed her sister partially because she felt it was good for both of them. Getting lost in her sister's mysterious past had given her something to focus on.

Jeniva looked out the window, watching people walk the New Orleans streets. The hotel she had chosen was only a block away from Bourbon St, and it was rumored that the beautiful hotel was haunted. Jeniva thought it would be a wonderful adventure and a cute play on her sister's birthday, but after leaving Iris's house she was starting to rethink her stance on being playfully spooky on her sister's Halloween birthday. She stared at the clock, deciding to try to shake the ominous feeling in her stomach and show her sister a good time for her birthday. She gently shook her sister.

"Maya, you want to start to get ready?" Jeniva gently asked as she rubbed her older sister's shoulder.

"I don't know. I think I might want to stay in." Maya spoke with her eyes still closed. The mental exhaustion she felt weighted her body down.

"I think we should have a good time, and then tomorrow we will change our tickets, fly home, and be done with all this stuff. Mom always went extra for your birthday. It's a tradition. We have to, so go get dressed." Jeniva smiled.

Maya laid against the bed not wanting to move. Visions of the night's events swarmed around her head. She didn't know if she had the energy to move, let alone party for her birthday. She opened her eyes and looked at her sister's pleading face.

They had both been through so much and if it will make her happy, then Maya was willing to do it.

"All right, we can go, but not too late okay. I'm starting to get my fill of this city already." That overwhelming feeling that hit Maya the moment she landed still buzzed within her. She walked towards the bathroom, briefly looking over her shoulder at her sister before closing the door to the bathroom.

Maya and Jeniva walked the crowded streets of New Orleans. The air was filled with jubilant energy. Some people wore costumes, others barely dressed, drinking from long cups with grenades at the end while running and dancing in the streets. Neither had ever experienced anything like it. Maya's eyes roamed the streets while sipping her drink. She wanted to enjoy her twenty-fifth birthday but her thoughts would not allow her.

They continued to walk and point. Her sister danced and flirted trying to pull her sister out of the funk she was in. They still hadn't talked about what happened at Iris Bissett's house, but she was trying to give her sister time to open up.

Maya...

A male's voice wafted through the air, landing on Maya's ears.

"Did you hear that?" Maya looked at her sister. She didn't know anyone here.

"Hear what?"

"Never mind," Maya shrugged her shoulders, then quickly dismissed her thoughts.

Maya...

She heard it again. She looked around to see if she could identify where the sound was coming from. Maya looked down the side street they were standing in front of. The street seemed to glow with lights as people she could barely make out partied and drank.

"What's down there?" Maya pointed towards the side street.

"There's nothing down there, just a dark alley." Jeniva's lip curled as she stared at her sister.

"No, you don't see that light. Look." Maya moved towards the alley. The lights and sounds calling to her. Jeniva grabbed her attempting to stop her.

"Maya, come on it's almost midnight, let's go into one of these bars and bring your birthday in right."

"It's plenty of people down there." Maya pointed. The urge pulling her down the street was strong. Maya insisted she saw people, Jeniva saw no one. Before Jeniva could protest Maya grabbed her hand and pulled her onto the dark empty street. Just as they crossed the intersection, lights and sounds began to buzz around the two. Jeniva struggled to make sense of what was happening. Moments ago she saw nothing but a dark street, now it was crowded with people.

Maya held on to her hand as they continued to walk. Her heart beat furiously as they whizzed between people.

"Maya," The voice she had been hearing was now closer to her than it had been previously. She searched around looking for the person that could be calling her name. Just as she turned forward she saw him. She had seen his face before but in her dreams. He walked slowly towards her as if he were floating on air. "Finally," He spoke just before stopping in front of her.

The handsome stranger reached for Maya's right hand, causing her to release the grasp she had on her sister.

"I've been waiting for you for so long. I was starting to wonder if you would ever hear my call." His deep brown almond-shaped eyes peered into her, causing a jolt of electricity to flood her entire body. His arms enveloped her as he pulled her near. "I'm Kaden, I am happy to finally meet you." He smiled. The masculine scent of his cologne invaded her senses. She was drawn to the man as if she had known him as if she had seen him before. Their bodies moved to the music that blasted throughout the street as she gazed into his eyes. Those deep chestnut brown eyes were familiar to her, she knew them, even though she could not recall when and where they had met.

For the first time in a long time, a smile spread across Maya's face. Being near him created a sense of calm in the midst of all the chaos she constantly felt. These feelings were inexplicable but intoxicating.

She looked back towards her sister for a nod of approval, but Jeniva was turning in circles looking for her sister. Maya could see her, but the moment she released her hand, Jeniva stood alone in complete darkness.

Chapter Ten

"Mayaaaaaaaaa!" Jeniva turned from left to right looking for Maya. Her heart pounded uncontrollably within her chest as she became dizzy with anxiety. With her mind a hazy fog, struggling to understand what just happened, Jeniva ventured further down the dark alley. She walked down the dark street frantically searching for Maya.

All the people that had just danced and drank in the streets were gone, and now there were only a few people, counting herself. Jeniva fell against the ground as she struggled to hold back the tears that threatened to stream from her eyes. Her breaths were labored and uncontrolled, she reached and grabbed the curb trying to steady herself.

"Fuuuuuuck!" She shouted into the empty street. Anger completely enveloping her. Her fist clenched as she shouted into the wind. "People don't just fucking disappear!" She yelled again into the night. She didn't care that that the handful of people that stood on the street with her was staring.

"Jeniva?" The unfamiliar voice called out to her in the darkness. Jeniva squinted to make out the person who was calling her name. Even though she was frightened out of her mind, she moved closer, praying it was someone who could help her. Not knowing how they would help or caring, Jeniva ventured closer to the sound of the voice.

"It's me, Christian. Iris' son," He moved closer to her, making himself visible to her.

"Christian?" She paused briefly wondering what he was doing here, but then quickly dismissed the thought. She looked up at him as the tears started to stream. Jeniva wasn't one to waste tears, if she was crying it meant she was truly heartbroken and in need.

"What's wrong, where's your sister?" He asked her while staring down the dark street. Jeniva looked at him, wanting to answer but not knowing how to explain the unexplainable. A cold chill washed over her as she hugged herself. She looked down at the black asphalt in search of the answers. She doubted he would believe her, the thought of saying it out loud seemed insane. Jeniva lifted her eyes and focused on him. She reasoned with herself. This was the man who claimed to be a "seer" and if he wanted her to believe that, she was sure that she couldn't possibly sound any crazier. She opened her mouth, hesitating at first, but then she decided to just go for it.

"She was standing right here," Jeniva pointed to the empty space beside her, "she was holding my hand and then she just disappeared into thin air. Just gone!" Jeniva shook her head uncontrollably as her soft curls swayed back and forth. "You can help me, please do your weird seer thing, please." Jeniva reached to grab him, pleading with him to help. As soon as her hands touched his, she was back in the center of the party. The empty alley was once again filled with people, their bodies dancing and sipping drinking while happily gyrating their bodies and grinding their hips. These people seemed to not have a care in the world, a feeling that had been elusive to Jeniva.

"Don't let go!" Christian cautioned.

"What the hell is going on?"

"This area is protected by a cloaking spell, only the gifted can see it."

"Gifted?"

"Yes," Christian stopped and faced Jeniva, understanding that all of this was new to her. The mysterious and occult to him was a way of life, he understood she wasn't from the South and she couldn't possibly understand their ways after only a few days. "When your sister held your hand, it opened the doorway for you, through her powers you saw what she saw. Do you understand?" Jeniva's nervousness didn't allow her to answer.

No, She thought.

"Just don't let go. I'll help you find your sister." Christian walked through the crowd of people, sipping on their own drinks that included no alcohol but would get you drunk with power. He closed his eyes trying to sense Maya. He inhaled and then slowly exhaled, concentrating on her, setting his intention on finding her in the sea of people before him. He was still linked to her from today's events. It was faint but it was there.

"What do you mean, you've been waiting for me?" Maya looked up at the handsome man, tracing her eyes over every inch of his face. The eyes, the smile, the brow, were all things she had seen before. He was the man she had dreamed about. Maya couldn't explain it but she was drawn to him. Ever since she landed there had been an abundance of things she couldn't explain, but her time in New Orleans had shown her there was a great deal more to this world than she understood.

Is it possible that I know this man, without knowing this man? Thoughts tumbled through her head as she waited for him to answer.

"Just what I said," the confident smile spread across his face as he watched her. "You really don't know do you?" He asked. He twirled her hair in his hands, knowing the answer before she spoke it.

"Know what?" Maya was captivated by the man. Her heart seemed to beat in unison with his. She could hear the rhythmic thumping in his chest as he pulled her closer to him.

"Close your eyes," he whispered in her ear as he pulled her body into his. "I know everything about you. And if you think hard enough you know me too."

Maya didn't understand how it was possible, but somehow she knew it was true. Their bodies swayed back and forth to a melody only the two of them could hear. Just as he had in her dream his hand slipped behind her head and pulled her into him. The anticipation of their lips touching caused a current of electricity to spark through her body. The closer he got, the greater the pull. Her eyes closed as their lips connected.

"Maya! What the hell?" Jeniva stood angrily staring at Maya. The scene seemed foreign to Jeniva. Maya hadn't seemed to be concerned or even notice that Jeniva had been separated from her.

Maya turned towards the sound of her sister's voice, pulling out of her trance-like state with the man in front of her. Jeniva reached for Maya's hand tearing her away from him. Her eyes became tiny slits as she stared at the strange man Maya was kissing. It wasn't like her sister to kiss strangers, but ever since landing in Louisiana, Maya hadn't been herself. With each passing minute, she was evolving into someone Jeniva couldn't predict or understand.

"Let's go!" Jeniva yelled while pulling Maya away. Christian looked at the man, their eyes locking in a war of wills. Christian's eyes were alive with fire, and then a flash of sorrow. His face twisted in determination. *Leave her alone, Kaden!* Christian thought as he continued to stare the man down. This wasn't their first encounter and he knew it wouldn't be the last.

"Make me," He laughed before turning slowly and then disappearing in the crowd.

Chapter Eleven

eniva fumed with anger as they walked back to the hotel in silence. Christian trailed behind them, watching over the two. He paid close attention to Maya. She was the source of so much power, and he didn't believe she comprehended the magnitude of the power she possessed.

"I got it from here," Jeniva said as she stopped just before they entered into the hotel, breaking the silence between the trio.

"I can come up, just make sure that guy didn't follow you guys, we can't be too careful with him," as Christian spoke the words a forceful wind blew through the thick humid air. Jeniva looked around feeling eery about all of today's events. Things were becoming much too weird for her.

"No offense, Christian, I appreciate you helping us out today, but this is getting way to strange for me. I don't want anything else to do with this freaky foolishness." Jeniva turned and entered the hotel, "Come on Maya."

Maya silently watched the exchange between the two of them, barely able to focus on their conversation. Her mind swarmed with thoughts of the man she had just met. It was evident to her that Christian knew who he was.

"I'm sorry, she's cranky. The man, the one I was dancing with, you knew him right?" She asked.

"Stay away from him Maya, with everything that's happening to you I know you have to believe now. He's trouble." Christian reached and grabbed her arm, attempting to connect with her, but when he touched her all he could feel was an icy shroud that had somehow enveloped her. A wall was up around her, and it would take more than his touch to penetrate it. He pulled his hand back and smiled. "If you need anything, ask." Christian's feet were planted firmly where he stood. His reluctance to leave was evident to both Maya and Jeniva.

"Maya!" Jeniva screamed from the lobby of the hotel, her tone dripped with impatience and annoyance. She wanted as much distance between them as she could get. The sooner they could get back on a plane, the better. Hearing the annoyance in Jeniva's voice, Maya waved her hand towards Christian and walked into the hotel towards her sister.

"What's your problem?" She said stopping in front of Jeniva. Her nose wrinkled as she looked down at her little sister.

"What do you mean what's my problem? You are the one that dragged me down some dark freaky street and disappeared on me."

"You were right behind me, I looked back and saw you standing there."

"Yeah, but I couldn't see you, and then I walk up on you about to shove your tongue down some stranger's throat. What the hell is wrong with you? Mom didn't raise us to be hoes, Maya." Jeniva spat as they exited the elevator and headed towards their room.

"So now I'm a hoe? Because I danced with someone? This was your idea to come down here not mine, remember. Now that I'm actually finding out something about my history you have a problem with that?" Maya was growing tired of Jeniva's hypocrisy. She, after all, was the one who pushed for this trip.

"Finding out about your history and going along with this witch bullshit are two different things!" Jeniva entered the room and threw her small crossbody purse onto her bed.

"I'm not going along with anything, I'm just trying to make sense of things. You have no idea what's going on in my head, and you haven't even tried to understand."

"Understand? I understand you've been seriously fucked up! This is too far Maya!" Jeniva walked into the bathroom and slammed the door. She stared at her reflection in the mirror, knowing that she had allowed words to slip from her lips to hurt her sister. But she just wanted to wake her up.

"This trip was a mistake." She said to her reflection. Jeniva thought about her parents. They would be disappointed in the way she talked to her sister. Jeniva softly slid the door open, cautiously peeping through the crack at her sister. She sat silently on the bed. Jeniva momentarily pondered what was on her mind. To her, it seemed that these most recent days had gone from bad to worse. Losing their parents had devastated them both, but on top of that Maya had found out her life was a well-woven lie. Instantly, feelings of remorse washed over Jeniva. She opened the door fully and stepped out.

"Maya," She spoke gently, attempting to ease into the conversation. Maya looked at her, her eyes were glossy with tears.

"I'm sorry about earlier. I'm sorry for talking to you the way that I did." Jeniva walked towards her and sat down on the bed. Maya looked at her but still hadn't spoken a word.

"It's fine,"

"No, it's not fine, I didn't have to talk to you the way I did. I just don't understand what's happening to you, Maya. None of this is like you." Jeniva decided to tell Maya how she was feeling. Maybe they could find some common ground and then move past this.

"I don't understand any of it either. Until a few days ago I didn't even think any of it was real." Maya finally spoke aloud her inner thoughts to her sister.

"Are you telling me now that you think this crap is real?" Jeniva responded in disbelief. She believed there had to be some reasonable explanation for the things that had happened. Magick wasn't real, and there was very little Maya could say that would convince her otherwise.

"Don't you? Look at everything. At Iris's house, I saw things. Things I can't explain. And that man, I know him. I've seen him. I've dreamt about him. If it's not real how can you explain that." Jeniva looked at the desperation in her sister's eyes.

Even though Jeniva had witnessed some equally questionable things, she knew there was an explanation. The more she pondered the thought the more she could explain it away, she had seen Criss Angel disappear and reappear in Vegas, levitate, and many other tricks, and for her, there was always a reason and this was no different.

"Yeah, things are strange, but we are in New Orleans, and it's Halloween. What if it's just all the power of suggestion? I mean now that I've had some time to think about it, how can any of this be real." Jeniva rationalized the events.

"All the strange things started before we ever got here." Maya thought of all the visions and feelings she was having. All of the times she could somehow hear what Jeniva was thinking had to be connected to this. She waited for Jeniva to say something but there was nothing between them but an awkward pause. Silence fell over the two, they both had no more words to explain what was happening.

"I think we've gotten as much information as we can. I'm

going to go get your gift from it's hiding place, and then try to get us a flight out of here as soon as possible." Jeniva spoke and then kissed her sister on her cheek. She wasn't used to having to take care of her, Maya was always so together, but she could see whatever she was dealing with, being here wasn't helping her get passed it.

Maya didn't speak, instead, she nodded her head in agreement. Jeniva left the room again. Just as she did Maya heard a soft knock on the door.

"Who's there?" She asked as she went towards the door and peeped out of the small peephole. A smile spread across her face as she slowly opened the door, and then closed it behind her.

"Happy Birthday to you! Happy Birthday to you!" Jeniva exited the bathroom with a small cupcake and gift bag in hand. "What the hell," Jeniva stopped dead in her tracks. The room was empty and Maya was nowhere to be found.

Chapter Twelve

His smooth chocolate skin seemed to shine in the moonlight as Maya walked down the street alongside him. Since the moment they met, he was all she could think about. So many questions swarmed around Maya's head. Even though she knew it was insane she had agreed to take this walk with him. She knew it was illogical, but the overwhelming pull she felt when around him was unbearable and she was completely unequipped to fight it.

"This is crazy," Maya's voice trembled as she spoke to him. Her words were soaked in anxiety. "I should really get back to my room. My sister will be worried."

"What's so crazy about us?" A smile spread across his face, exposing his perfect white teeth. The contrast of his deep skin and his ivory smile contributed to his handsome features.

"Me, here with you, honestly I don't know you."

"But you do," Maya paused staring at him. His words rang with more truth than he knew. She would never admit to him that she had dreamed of his face before they met. She couldn't explain any of the things that were happening to her, and the struggle of trying to rationalize the illogical kept her brain in a constant fog.

"I know you are confused, but listen. Listen, " Kaden paused to take her hand. "Close your eyes," His deep baritone voice was soft and kind as he spoke to her. She did as he requested. As she held his hands the noise of the streets seemed to disappear. It was silence and the only thing audible to her was the beating of their hearts. The soft thumps seemed to beat in unison.

Can you hear me? His voice invaded her head. *Don't answer with your lips, speak to me with your mind.*

Yes, I hear you. Maya responded. Her heart raced as her mind attempted to connect the dots of what was happening. She had heard voices in her head before.

You can control it. You're special Maya, lean into your powers. Kaden's words tumbled around in her head. Maya released his hands and looked into his eyes.

"You're making me uncomfortable." Maya stepped back from Kaden. His presence was overwhelming. He was so close, she could feel the heat of his breath as he breathed. "Kaden, right?" This was the first time that Maya had spoken his name.

"Right," He gently pushed her curls from her face and cupped the back of her head. Her body softened and then tensed.

"I think it's time for me to go back."

"Just a few more minutes with you, I've waited a long time for this moment." The sultriness in his voice caused her legs to shift from side to side. "Let me show you more about our city." Kaden grabbed her hand as they continued to walk.

"You keep saying you know me, how is that even possible?" Maya wanted to know what he thought he knew about her. She had finally admitted to herself that things weren't making any sense without entertaining the thought of some sort of magick. Maybe he knew about her family, maybe more of where she came from.

"There are a lot of possibilities in this world if you just open your eye to them."

"That guy, Christian, his mom told me that my mom was some type of voodoo witch or something and that I'm one too." As the words rolled off her lips she realized how crazy it sounded.

"Did you believe it?"

"I don't know what to believe."

"You know what's in your heart." Kaden stopped, taking Maya's hands into his as he stared into her eyes. "Everything you need to know is already with you." Maya looked down at her feet as she spoke, his touch was oddly comforting to her.

"You're being very nice, but you don't understand what's been going on with me. I feel like I'm losing my mind." Kaden looked at her, his eyes filling with compassion and concern. His eyes were deep pools of amber, pulling her in deeper the more she looked at them. Heat rose from every pore of her body as he looked her over. Maya's eyes shifted towards the ground, no longer able to withstand the intensity of his stare.

"Maya, look at me," Kaden paused and waited for Maya to lift her head. Once their eyes connected, he continued, "Don't be scared of who you are, of what we are. We have the power to change lives. Let me show you," Kaden pulled her hands in towards his chest. "My car's right over here."

Kaden began to lead her towards the black Mercedes. The sleek curves of the car mesmerized Maya. She knew she shouldn't be going but she trusted him. To her, this was a chance to find out more about where and what she came from. Weeks ago a world like this did not exist.

Maya slipped inside of the car and rode in silence. Her eyes darted to the left, constantly stealing glances of his ebony skin that seemed to glow in the moonlight. She shifted in her seat enthralled by the sight of him. Everything about him was intriguing. The constant pull she felt when near him was as strong as a magnet, like two opposite ends drawn to each other with unyielding force.

"So if I'm a witch," her voice trembled with each word she spoke, "then you must be one too. Are you a, a, witch?" Maya broke the silence in the car. Kaden chuckled as he glanced her way.

"I prefer the word conjurer," He spoke, glancing at her. To Kaden, Maya appeared scared, vulnerable.

"Conjurer," Maya let the words roll off her lips, not fully understanding its meaning.

"So what's the difference?"

"I know you weren't raised here, so there are a lot of things you don't understand about what you are. But what we do is magick, it's manifestation, with the help of our ancestors and the elements." Maya heard the words but couldn't quite comprehend what he was saying. The only thing she knew about witches or magick was what she saw in the movies. None of it was real, but everything she had experienced had told her that none of what she thought was true.

"Do you know anything about my family," Maya asked as the car rolled to a stop in front of a two-story house deep in the woods. There didn't seem to be anyone around for miles.

"I know something happened and none of them survived. I can help you."

"Iris said she could help me but she just ended up confusing me even more."

"But when I say I can help you, I mean it. I wouldn't be so quick to trust them. She's been obsessed with your family for years."

Maya locked eyes with Kaden and instantly trusted him. She didn't understand why she did, she just knew she could.

"Come on, let's go in." He said as they exited the car. He reached to grab her hand as they walked towards the open door. The light from within seemed to illuminate with a yellow glow. She could feel the energy surge from the house. She stopped, her heart beating uncontrollably.

"It's okay," Kaden's deep voice was steeped with concern.

"I feel . . ."

"It's the energy from the house you feel. Don't be scared. If I do know anything about your mother, I hear she wasn't afraid of anything, and if you plan to find out something about them, it's going to be inside these walls."

She gripped his hand again, deathly tight, and continued to walk inside. Kaden pulled her close to him. She could feel the heat from his body, and it calmed her.

Her eyes roamed the room as they walked inside, there were two women inside who all seemed close to Kaden's age and an older woman sat in the corner. Her hair was stark white falling into two long braids that ended at her waist. She sat quietly in the corner as the other women took in the sight of Maya, their eyes greedily devouring her. Everyone was silent as Kaden and Maya moved through the room towards the woman in the back.

"These are my sisters, and my grandmother. They will help me guide you." Kaden said as he guided her to a chair next to his grandmother.

"This is her," Kaden smiled at the woman who sat with her back to Maya. Her frame was small and feeble. Maya looked at her wrinkled hands bent with arthritis and waited for the woman to acknowledge her presence. The silence in the room was paralyzing. Maya was afraid to speak so she sat completely still.

The woman slowly turned to face Maya, her hand creeping

towards Maya's open palm on the table. The old woman's milky white eyes connected with Maya's. When her hands touched Maya, she was flooded with heat that Maya was starting to feel familiar whenever something strange was about to happen.

"C'est la bonne. It's her." The old woman said before getting up from her chair and walking away.

Chapter Thirteen

Maya sat silently next to Kaden's sisters. She watched as people came into the home, looking for help with concerns ranging from money to help to hexes. An entirely new world was opening up to her. Kaden walked towards the group of women with a smile spread across his face.

"Do you want to help me with a spell?" He leaned over and whispered in her ear.

"Yes," Maya was eager to learn as much as she possibly could. She got up and followed Kaden. Most of the time they had been on the bottom floor, but she followed him upstairs, staying close behind. Kaden walked into a dimly lit room that had a table with a spread of water, herbs, and oils. She walked across the room and took a seat.

"Wash your hands," Kaden commanded. Maya complied and dipped her hands in the water, letting the room temperature liquid slip through her fingertips. "Even though we have our gifts, a lot of our work is elemental magick, air, earth, fire, and water." Kaden paused to light a stick of incense.

Maya watched as he mixed and poured, talking her through everything he was doing. With each word, he spoke she felt more comfortable with the word magick.

"So what about all the other stuff, the voices I hear, the visions I have?" Maya asked.

"You were born with those abilities. From the things I do know both your mother and father were very powerful, you received gifts from both. Just like my family. We all have our gifts, some of us were born with natural ability. That's why I can communicate with you through your thoughts, my sister, Naya is clairvoyant and Naima has the ability to hear communicate with the dead. But you're like me, we were born able to harness all of these things." Kaden finished.

"And what happened to all my relatives?" Maya asked. She was longing to connect with someone from her bloodline.

"I don't know, but I can help you find out." As Kaden spoke he moved towards Maya. He reached for her hand and pulled her from her chair and into him.

She looked up at him, pushing herself as close to him as possible. The heat again rose from his body, causing tiny beads of sweat to run down her back. Her eyes fluttered as she became intoxicated with the smell of him. She inhaled as his lips connected to hers and they kissed.

His tongue slipped between her lips, softly parting her mouth. His hands enveloped her, and then slowly exploring her soft supple skin. Her long legs quivered with each touch.

I shouldn't be doing this

Maya thought as he continued to press his body into hers.

Why not?

She heard his voice in her thoughts. The fact that they could communicate in such a way excited her. Kaden guided her to the bed and pushed her on top of it.

"But I barely know you." Maya hesitated.

"But you do...know me," He whispered as he slid his tongue down her long slender neck, landing on her shoulders and planting a kiss.

"Mmmmm," She moaned releasing sounds of desire. They landed on a bed that was in the room. Kaden's hands slipped beneath her shirt and grasped her breast, cupping them in his hand while gently teasing her nipple through the soft fabric of her bra. Her back arched as she felt his hardness press against her. Kaden started to remove her clothes and then his, while gently kissing her. His touch felt just as it had when she dreamed of him. Her pulse quicken, causing a heated fire that surged through her. The web of desire was so strong, she could concentrate on nothing but having him inside of her. The air hummed thick with the magick the two created.

Kaden pushed her legs back and slid between her thighs, nuzzling his face between her folds. His tongue lightly licked, pushing it between her lips and sampling her sweetness. He was drowning in her taste, the faster his tongue move the wetter she became. Moisture dripped down his chin as he licked every ounce of her sweetness. Her hands rubbed across the top of his head as his tongue darted in and out of her. The pressure was building inside of her. Kaden's tongue slid further inside, opening her folds, applying more pressure to her clitoris. He sucked and nibbled, then slowly brought his hands to her center and slid them deep inside of her.

Maya arched her back as his fingers played inside of her. His fingers swirled inside, moving back and forth, causing the blazing fire that was already lit within her to explode.

"That feels. . .mmmmm" She moaned. The louder her moans became the more aggressive he became. Wetness poured from between her thighs as he continued sucking. Maya rolled her hips as he made a continuous come hither motion with his fingers. Her nipples hardened as her body began to throb.

"Ummmm, you're gonna make me cum," Maya released softly. He continued stroking her softest parts, bringing her closer and closer to orgasm, but not allowing her that release. Her body tensed and Kaden withdrew his fingers and in one fluid motion, he was inside.

Maya released a breath as he slid inside of her, his thickness stretching her, causing her both pleasure and pain. His erection filled her, slowly chipping away all her inhibitions, leaving her with only her desire for him. Kaden's strokes were deep and deliberate, giving her all of him with each and every motion. Pressure tapped against her clit, exciting her more each time he plunged within her. She was hungry for more of him, all of him. Maya pushed her body forward, wrapping her shapely legs around his waist, tightening and pulling him further into her.

"You're mine," he groaned as he pounded against her body. Kaden laid claims on her, lost in the depth of her pleasure, his body was overtaken with lust. Maya heard his demand. His claims on her body turned her on even more. She lifted her hips, grinding her clit against him.

Kaden pushed her legs back as far as they could go and braced himself on her thighs. Her body trembled as the pressure from his strokes hit her stomach. He stroked harder, faster, deeper as her body gave in to him.

"Cum for me baby, cum with me," He demanded of her and her body responded.

"Daaaaaaamn," Maya screamed as her body convulsed with pleasure as she moisture streamed from inside of her. The bed shook with intensity shifting the bed out of its position, exposing the carved markings beneath the post.

"That's it baby, cum all over my dick!" Kaden grumbled as he released inside of her. The scratches in the floorboards began to glow. They breathed heavily as their bodies landed against the bed.

"I've never done that," Maya said.

"Which part?" Kaden laughed.

"I've never had an orgasm like that." Maya felt somewhat exposed.

"We will have a lot of first," Kaden responded.

Maya didn't know how to take that, or to any of what was happening for that matter.

"I probably should be getting back to my sister," Maya said. Kaden stared at her for a moment before speaking. She tried to read his thoughts like he showed her earlier, but she couldn't. There was only silence.

"Okay, get dressed I will take you back."

They began to put on their clothes and headed back downstairs. Once they made it back to the first floor, Kaden grabbed his keys.

"Wait here a minute," he said, "let me say goodbye to my grandmother."

Maya waited patiently as he said his goodbyes. Kaden walked towards the back of the house to his grandmother's room. He knocked softly against the door.

"Come in," She said, barely above a whisper. He entered the room, she sat on her bed combing her long tresses, never turning towards his direction.

"It's done," Kaden said as he peeked into the room. She shook her head and continued to comb her hair as he left and closed the door.

Chapter Fourteen

The loud thump against the door jolted Jeniva from her seat. She moved quickly towards the door and looked out the peephole. Jeniva briefly watched as Iris seemed to have a conversation with someone that wasn't there. She shook her head and dismissed the actions of the odd woman, in this moment she had more important things to deal with.

"I didn't know who to call," she said as she opened the door. Iris and Christian stepped inside of the hotel room. "And I didn't want to leave in case she came back. Thank you guys for coming." Jeniva looked as if she hadn't slept for days. Her hair was tousled and her clothes were disheveled.

"Tell us what happened," Iris wasted no time trying to get the facts of what was going on.

"I don't know why she left. It started after that weird party," Jeniva made eye contact with Christian before continuing, "you remember the one that kept disappearing." Iris turned towards her son, raising an eyebrow as their eyes locked.

"It was cloaked," He turned to his mom before waving his

hand, "okay and then what I brought you guys back, everything seemed fine so what happened?" Christian stressed his words. His eyebrows furrowed as he recounted the night, desperately trying to figure out what he could have possibly missed. He had been sure that no one was in or around the hotel before leaving. He had guarded the room long enough to over hear their argument, and he didn't leave until everything seemed to be resolved. He scratched his head, impatiently waiting for her to continue.

"Well, we had an argument, because she was acting so damn strange. All over somebody she didn't even know, and she completely left me alone in a dark street. I was pissed. But I thought we made up, went to go get her gift, and came out and she was gone."

"Gone," Iris repeated.

"Yes, just fuckin' up and disappeared. This isn't like her. She doesn't just disappear. Something had to happen to her." Jeniva flopped against the sofa in the seating area.

"She didn't just disappear," Iris said. Someone else has been here. She looked around the room, closing her eyes. She held her hands up, palms outward as she felt the energy in the room. Different people left different energies, what she was feeling was a dark presence, familiar, but dark.

"What the hell is she doing?" Jeniva jumped up from her seat. "I need help and she's closing her eyes and humming. What the fuck is wrong with you people my sister is missing. We don't know anything about this damn city and she's out there, alone . . ."

Iris waved her hand to silence Jeniva. She understood her passion but not her impatience. "Be quiet, I'm trying to read the energy in this room," She said as she continued to walk around the room counter-clockwise, searching for anything left by whomever or whatever took Maya.

"Christian, what did you see when you left?" Iris quizzed.

"Nothing, they were safe,"

"Obviously they weren't." Iris hissed through clenched teeth. The sound of the door opening disturbed the trio. They all faced the opening door as Maya entered into the room.

"Where the hell have you been?" Jeniva bolted towards her sister. "And you leave without telling anyone with who or where you were going?"

"Calm down Niva, I just took a walk with Kaden. I haven't even been gone that long."

"Maya? Really? You haven't been gone that long? You've been gone for three damn days! I don't know what's wrong with you but this shit has got to stop."

"Three days, that doesn't make any sense." Maya's mind raced. It had only been a few hours so why would Jeniva say she's been gone for days. She walked towards the nightstand and picked up her iPhone to look at the date. She had been so surprised when Kaden stopped by she had forgotten to grab it and take it with her.

Maya glanced down at the date. Her face twisted in confusion as the phone slipped from her hand and bounced against the plush carpeting before landing face down against the floor. It didn't make any sense, how had she been gone for three days yet it felt like only a few hours. Iris saw the confusion in her face and moved towards her, trying to grab her hand. Her icy fingertips grazed Maya, causing her to pull away.

"Where did he take you?" Iris asked.

"I um, his family home. He was nice to me, he's helping me to understand who I am." Maya said defensively. She didn't like how the woman was acting.

"Open your mouth," Iris demanded.

"No, move back." Maya pushed her back. "Why are they even here Jeniva?"

"I didn't know who else to call Maya! You disappeared ..."

"They put something on you!" Iris said, interrupting the

argument that was erupting between the sisters. Iris could feel it, the more she looked at Maya the more she could see the roots taking hold of her. "Open your mouth." Iris didn't give her the chance to pull back. She reached up towards Maya's chin and pulled her mouth open. She could see the darkness in the back of her throat slowly creeping through her. Iris jumped back at the sight, releasing her grasp on Maya.

"Go get my bag out of the car Christian." Iris stepped back, her eyes never leaving Maya. "You shouldn't have left with him, girl." She mumbled. The darkness brewing inside her was a time bomb, waiting for the perfect time to explode. Iris didn't know what she could do or it was too late to undo what had already been done.

"What's going on Iris?"

"Something dark has her," Iris said, still staring at Maya. Jeniva rolled her eyes. She was tired of all the "magick" talk, she was done with all of their useless metaphors.

"Stop it, nothing dark has me, I went out with someone I like. Someone like me, who can help me understand who and what I am. That's more than you can do." Maya looked Iris up and down.

"You can't trust him, everything is not what it seems."

"Funny thing is he said that I can't trust you! That you were just some crazy nut obsessed with what happened to me."

"That's what he wants you to think."

"No, he's not the one half telling me stuff and doing crazy shit but not telling me a damn thing. You are. He was honest, he showed me how to do things, the only thing you've managed to help with was giving me a headache and playing mind games with me." Fury built within Maya, it seemed that since she had arrived in this city the only people that had been remotely honest with her had been Kaden and his family. "And besides, his grandmother is going to help me with getting real answers to who my family is."

"His grandmother?" Iris mumbled. Maya's chest rose with each heated breath. Her skin burned at all the accusations that were hurled her way.

"Yes, no one did anything to me. Leave!"

"Let me help you,"

"I don't need your help"

Christian entered the room, just as Maya spoke those words. The look on his mother's face told him everything he needed to know about what happened. It was obvious Maya was refusing her help. Iris walked over to the bag Christian brought in and began to sift through it. She pulled out a blue bundle tied with a ribbon.

"You need our help more than you know," Iris placed the bag in Maya's hand. "hopefully this gris-gris can protect you; before you get in too deep to get yourself out." Iris closed Maya's hand over the small cloth bag that she had constructed for protection. "Let's go, Christian, we've done all we can do for now."

Iris and Christian walked out of the door, leaving a confused Jeniva and a seething Maya in the room.

"So is that it? We just let this happen?" Christian quizzed.

"We're not letting anything just happen, she'll come back, until then, we keep trying to protect her, as we always have, from afar."

Chapter Fifteen

"I don't understand why you let her leave." The woman's raspy voice was barely audible in the dark-room. Kaden sat at the edge of the bed, listening. He reached and grabbed her hand. Her skin felt fragile to his touch. He squeezed her feeble hand tenderly as their eyes connected. He leaned in and kissed the one tear that rolled from her left eye, letting the salty drops land on his lips.

"We have to be patient," Kaden said, trying to reassure her. "Just hold on a little longer, and this will all be over soon."

"That's a lot easier for you to say, you don't have to deal with any of this. I'm old now. I've never been old, and my body is giving up. I can't go backward and I can't move forward." The elderly woman's voice cracked as she continued to speak, "I'm stuck," Kaden wrapped his hands around her wanting to console her. "She has to be here." Her eyes were deep pools of despair.

"I know, but we still have four more days to complete the ritual. Let me worry about getting her here. Just hang on." He gently kissed her on the cheek before getting up and leaving the room. He hated seeing her like this, she was once such a vibrant woman, filled with energy and now he was watching her wither away. Sadness first and then guilt washed over him as he walked back to the front of the house.

Since taking Maya back to her hotel room, he hadn't been able to get her off of his mind. Something about her naive, aloofness, and eagerness to learn from him had struck something in him he hadn't felt for a long time. The newness of it all gave him a feeling of exhilaration, it was pure excitement every time he saw her. He toyed with the idea of psychically connecting with her as he had done before in her dreams just to see her again. Kaden shook his head from side to side, dismissing the thoughts. Kaden needed to get her out of his head. Once he made it back to the front room, he noticed Naima sitting silently on the sofa with her feet tucked beneath her.

"Daddy," she turned towards him as soon as she sensed him in the room. "How is mama?" She asked. Naima had always been his sensitive child, the one that held on tightly to both her parents and would be devastated if she had to let either one of them go.

"As best as she can be love." He answered sitting next to her on the black cushy sofa. He pulled her close and gave her a fatherly hug. He wanted nothing more at this moment than to calm his daughter and let her know that things would be okay.

"How much longer does she have?" Her eyes welled over with tears, "I've never seen her this weak before."

"If we don't complete the spell within the next four days, she won't make it. The body is giving up on her."

"Why couldn't we complete it when she was here?" Naima looked at her father, eagerly awaiting his reply.

"You know it takes time to build the power and intention necessary for this spell. If we rush it, it might not be successful."

Kaden responded. These were all things that his daughters knew, this wasn't their first time completing the ritual, but Naima needed to hear it again.

Naima fell against his shoulder and let out a flood of tears. Pretending that her father was her brother had come easy for her, each time they transferred it was different, but they were always healthy. This was the first time she thought she could actually lose her mother.

"What are we going to do?" Naya entered the room.

"Whatever we have to do chere, whatever we have to." Kaden stood, "I'm going out for a while, make sure she has everything she needs. I'll be back." Kaden knew it was time to act.

Maya lay sleeping in the bed while Jeniva made sure all of their bags were packed. She spent the entire afternoon on the phone making arrangements to leave as soon as possible. As far as Jeniva was concerned she was done with whatever this place had to offer. Her sister hadn't been herself since they got there.

I wish you were here mom and dad. Jeniva couldn't help but think of her parents. There was nothing they couldn't help her solve and now that they were gone, she and her sister were all alone, left with a mess of life that neither of them knew the first thing about maneuvering through. She let out a long sigh and continued to throw things into the open cases.

Maya began to toss and turn in the bed. Her mind flooded with thoughts of Kaden. An electric ball of fire flooded her nerve endings with each flash of his face. It's as if he knew every single part of her. She tossed from side to side, her legs kicking the sheets away from her heated skin. Misty smoke flooded her thoughts before she saw herself on a beach, the same beach Kaden had initially entered her dreams.

She could feel the warm wet sand beneath her bare feet as she walked towards him. The wind blew softly caressing her bare skin.

"Kaden," He turned to face her. His naked skin glistening in the sunny skies of her fantasy. Her eyes devoured the sight of him. His deep mahogany flesh was addictive and she wanted to savor it over and over again.

"Is this a dream?"

"Does it feel like one?" He asked.

"No," As she spoke his lips landed against hers. His kiss was passionate and deep. He softly swirled his tongue, savoring the taste of her.

"Why did you leave me?" Kaden asked between planting kisses on her lips. His hands slipped around her waist. He stiffened with arousal. He wanted her. Maya's arms wrapped around him and she kissed him back, remembering the heat he had ignited within her. Moans slipped from her lips as her lips below became wet and throbbed with desire.

"Maya!" Jeniva screamed. Maya woke up, confused from her dream. Her body still felt the lingering effects of dreaming of his touch.

"You need to get up and get ready we're leaving." Jeniva frowned while she watched Maya struggle to gain her composure.

"Jeniva, I'm not ready to go. You leave." Maya responded. She got up from the bed and walked to the window. She could sense his presence before she ever saw him. Kaden was standing in the street looking up at her. She grabbed her shoes and phone and headed towards the door. "Have a safe flight, call me when you make it home. I will be fine here."

Maya left the room leaving Jeniva speechless. She was tired of trying to explain to her sister what she was feeling and felt it was better for her to go back to Washington, and she could stay here, around people who understood her. She bolted out the door and down the stairs, not bothering to wait for the elevator.

The need to be near him was strong, to try to fight it was useless.

"You came to see me?" She asked Kaden as she walked outside of the hotel.

"I don't plan on letting you out of my sight." Kaden's lips widened into a sensual smile as he wrapped his arms around Maya.

Chapter Sixteen

"She's got to be out of her got damn mind!" Jeniva raced downstairs behind Maya. "Maya!" She called as she watched her sister slip through the opening glass door. Just as she walked outside she saw her embracing the man from the street party. His eyes were black pools of darkness as they locked with hers. The smile that was initially on his face spread into a straight line. His expression shot terror through Jeniva.

Jeniva attempted to get closer to Maya, but her feet felt as heavy as lead as she attempted to stop her sister from leaving with him.

"Ma..." Jeniva's voice cracked as she struggled to call out for her sister. She coughed relentlessly as she struggled to get her sister's attention. The harder she tried the more she choked on the words she tried to say.

Maya never noticed her sister behind her. The thought of spending more time with Kaden and learning everything he had to offer excited her.

"Did you ask your grandmother about what she knew?" She

asked Kaden, thrilled that he could be here to share some good news with her.

"Yes, she's feeling better and wants to talk to you." Kaden led her to his car and opened the door for her. Maya slipped in.

"I can't believe that I might finally have some answers to some of my questions. Do you know the story?"

"I know bits and pieces it was before my time," he laughed.

"I know you're just a little older than me so I know you weren't around then, but I'm just finding so much out. The one question that's been stuck in my head has been why?" Maya got quiet, fearful that she may be talking too much. They rode in silence to the home she had just left a day ago. As they pulled into the gravel driveway her heart skipped a beat.

Am I really this happy to be back here? Maya thought to herself. She opened her car door and headed to the front door. Unlike her last encounter, she wasn't scared to enter. She could feel the energy vibrations surrounding the property but it was a welcomed comfort. She walked into the house and greeted her new found friends, Naima and Naya sat on the sofa. They both waved and continued watching the show they were glued to.

"My grandmother is in the back," Kaden led her to the back of the house where the woman from the night before sat quietly at the table. Her long silver hair hung loose against her back. She turned towards them as they entered.

"Hello Maya," She said looking in the direction of Maya, but her eyes void of any sight.

"Hello," Maya took a seat in the chair in front of her.

"We didn't talk much the other night, my name is Delphine." She touched Maya's hand and smiled. A chill traveled through Maya's body as the woman held her hand. "I understand you have some questions."

"Yes, I'm just looking for anyone who can help me with information about my family, I don't know much. My parents, who I just found out were my adoptive parents left me a video and articles about my actual birth, but I've searched and searched and everything comes up a dead end."

"Your mother was the Puissant girl right, that killed herself in a cemetery," Delphine spoke.

"Yes," Hearing someone say those things aloud didn't feel good to Maya. So much mystery surrounded her birth and mother's death and this woman stating it so boldly and bluntly made her uncomfortable.

"I know a little, I knew your family, your mother's mother. It wasn't many of them left, and by the time your mother did what she did, there weren't any of the Puissant's left." Delphine paused to take a sip of her coffee, "Rumor is, yall's family was hexed."

"The reporter I talked to said my mother was running through the street the day she gave birth to me, and she helped me have a vision of a fight with her and my dad, do you know why they were, uh, hexed?" Maya asked, even though words like hexed and cursed were foreign to her, she wanted to know more. Delphine became silent and sipped her coffee. Maya was hanging on her every word, wanting to know as much as she could about her roots. Now that the fire had been lit, she wanted to soak up as much knowledge of her family as she could.

"I'm tired," She finally spoke, "Naya, take me to lie down." She called. Maya was disappointed that she had ended the conversation so abruptly. She looked at Kaden, who simply shrugged his shoulders.

"Let's take a walk in the back, we can practice more." Kaden took her to the backdoor and grabbed a blanket as they walked outside into the warm fall air.

"I'm sorry she couldn't answer more," Kaden said as they walked along the curved pathway leading to a small lake. The outside air gently whipped across their skin. Maya felt at peace anytime she was near Kaden, add the calm that nature provided and Maya was the happiest she had been in weeks.

"It's okay, I appreciate everything you're trying to help me with, um," Maya bit her lip, "I wonder if you guys can do a spell like Iris, one that will help me see more of my parents' past."

"We can try," Kaden grabbed her hand as they walked. Maya allowed him to pull her into him, she welcomed it. Once they reached the lake he spread the blanket across the grass and they had a seat.

"Let's practice your telepathy. It's quiet here so there won't be any other distractions." Kaden said, looking at Maya. For the first time, he actually took in her beauty, her delicate features, and the soft smile that spread across her face when she was unsure. Maya crossed her legs beneath her and closed her eyes. She had attempted this once before and had been unsuccessful.

"Concentrate and relax," Kaden instructed. The wind blew, carrying the soft scent of the fragrance she wore through the air.

Damn, she smells good.

I do? Maya thought, a sly smile spreading across her face. She had done it.

Yes.

So what else have you noticed about me? Maya's eyes narrowed as her long lashes fluttered. Her skin burned bright red as she thought about the question.

That I love the way I feel when I'm around you.

His response caught Maya off guard. She was feeling the same way, intoxicated by his presence in every way.

I love the way I feel kissing you...I love the way I feel inside of you.

Kaden moved closer to Maya with each word he thought. Her skin was heated and red from the southern heat that beamed down on her. He kissed her, slowly leaning her back against the blanket. His kisses even though eager, were gentle. Kaden's fingertips danced on her skin.

Maya's back arched with each touch. Her hands wrapped around his neck pulling him into her. Kaden ran his tongue down her neck, greedily tasting her skin. His mouth found her breast. Using his teeth he pulled the soft fabric away to expose her nipples. The hardened soft brown buds thrilled him even more. Her energy radiated from her and Kaden wanted to savor every ounce of her. He took her breast into his mouth, sucking softly while running his tongue in small circles.

Mmmmm, I want you

Kaden heard Maya loud and clear. He slipped his pants off and flipped Maya over, ripping her panties from beneath the dress she wore. Soft pants escaped her lips as she felt tiny kisses against her thighs. Kaden pushed her legs open and began tasting her from behind. His tongue danced across her clitoris, causing a flood of wetness. He grabbed her by her hips and pulled her to her knees as he continued to taste. Kaden was determined to sip every ounce of her sugary sweet nectar.

He pushed her back against the blanket and kissed her neck as he slid inside her from behind. Her stomach pressed against the blanket, Maya was his prisoner as he stroked her deeply. His hands found hers as their fingertips intertwined. Kaden pushed deep inside of her as wetness dripped from her. Maya arched her back, wanting to receive as much of him as she possibly could.

Eager to please Maya, Kaden pulled her to her back to knees. He pushed her head down and grabbed her cheeks, spreading them so he could push as deep as she could handle. Maya's hips rolled, meeting him stroke for stroke. Her supple c-cups bounced with intensity as her body throbbed with excitement, on the verge of release.

Baby

Yes

I'm

I know, cum with me!

Maya released a flood of wetness as Kaden shuddered with pleasure from the intensity of their orgasm. Kaden fell against the blanket on his back, and Maya landed on her stomach, both completely drained from the intensity of their lovemaking.

Kaden closed his eyes, blocking his thoughts. He didn't understand what it was about her that fiercely drew him to her.

"Kaden! Kadeeeeeen!" He could hear Naya's voice calling from a distance. Kaden grabbed his pants and stepped into them, trying to dress before Naya walked upon them. He was buttoning his pants just as she appeared. Naya stepped back as she took in the sight of the two. Her eyes threw daggers at Kaden, wondering what he could be thinking.

"Yes, Naya what is it?" Kaden's voice was dripping with anger.

"She needs you," Naya shot back, looking Maya up and down before turning around and walking away.

Maya watched the exchange, embarrassed that Naya walked up on them, but confused about her anger.

"Go, I'll grab the blanket and find my way back to the house," Maya said, trying to be helpful. It was evident to her that Naya was upset with him and he didn't want to give her our Delphine any reason to be upset. They had all been so nice to her, she didn't want to seem ungrateful.

"Okay," Kaden he leaned down and kissed Maya before heading back to the house. Maya lay against the blanket staring at the sky, the stillness of the moment calming her. She was finally starting to feel like things were becoming normal or as close to normal as they could be.

"Maya..." A voice whispered. The wind blew softly as Maya sat up looking around. There was no one there.

"Maya. . ."

She turned from side to side as she again heard the call of

her name. From the water, a figure of a woman rose. Maya watched as the ghostly figured moved towards her and then hovered over the edge of the lake.

"Don't be scared, I don't have long, it takes a lot of energy to cross into the land of the living, but I have to warn you, leave." She said. Maya wanted to run but decided not to. She wanted to learn and that couldn't happen if she ran or fainted every time something out of the ordinary happened.

"Who are you?" Maya asked.

"Baby, I'm your mother. I've been trying to make contact with you for months. This, baby, this ain't right, chere. You have to leave and go back home. These people mean you no good." She said. "I tried to protect you from this . . ."

"Protect me? How when you left me! Why did you leave me?" Maya shouted, her anger bubbling to the surface.

"I didn't want to leave you, but it was the only way I knew to protect you, and Anthony and Grace were there to protect you also. I made a mistake that day with your binding. They were never supposed to find you, but because I didn't bury it, as soon as it began to unravel your powers surfaced. That's how they were able to find you. And your parent's accident was no accident, they needed your parents out the way, can't you see?"

"Who are they? The only person who has hurt me is you, so no I don't see . . ."

"You have to leave!" The apparition floated forward, "Please." It floated closer to Maya and then disappeared, dropping the water that formed its shape before completely vanishing. Maya searched again for the figure but it was gone.

Her heart pounded like a drum inside of her chest. Heat surged through her body as a torrent of thoughts flooded her mind.

"Why does everyone want to keep me away from the one thing that was making life worth living for me at the moment?" Maya spoke aloud.

She defiantly jumped up from her seated position, grabbing and folding the blanket and heading back to the house. There was no way anyone was going to tell her when to leave, especially not someone who couldn't be bothered to stick around and raise her.

Chapter Seventeen

The gravel crunched beneath the tires as Jeniva sped down the long driveway leading to Iris's house. She hit the breaks as she neared the front bringing the vehicle to an abrupt stop. Jeniva wasted no time getting out of the car and making her way to the front door. She slammed her hand against the large wooden door, beating continuously until someone to answer.

"Hey come in," Christian said as he opened the door. Jeniva pushed past him.

"I didn't know who else to call, I didn't think the police would believe me when I said some magick witch guy took my sister." Jeniva was a bundle of nerves. She couldn't get the menacing sight of his face out of her mind.

"Calm down," Iris appeared from the other room.

"I can't calm down, what don't you understand about he took my sister." Jeniva's eyes bulged as she watched Iris in confusion. She didn't like the woman at all but she needed her help. She needed to find her sister and persuade her to go home.

"Calm down and tell me what happened."

"After you left, she went into some type of sleep trance, I don't know what it was because her eyes fluttered from open to close. She tossed in the bed so much that I woke her up and told her to get her stuff we were leaving. I don't know what made her do it, but she walked over to the window, looked out, and just left. She told me to go back home she was staying." Jeniva recounted the events.

"So this dream she was having did she say anything that you could understand?"

"No, it was all gibberish. So I tried to follow her, I called to her but my voice was gone. The words wouldn't come out, and then that's when I saw her hugging that Kaden guy, and the look. The look he gave me scared the shit out of me." Chills shot up the back of Jeniva's neck, making the hairs stand at attention. "Look Iris, I know you know more than you're letting on! You're going to have to start giving me some answers."

Jeniva was tired of playing games with these people. Nothing had made any sense to her and she could see if from the beginning this old lady was holding back and now her sister was out there, with God knows who doing who knows what. The room became silent, Iris not immediately answering, choosing her words carefully.

"Sit down," Iris motioned. "I only want to help your sister. Understand, how she feels. Everything is new to her, unloading all of it on her at one time is not the way. My mission is only to protect her."

"Mission, lady you sound crazy."

"Jeniva, after all, you have seen, how can any of this sound crazy to you. What you are not understanding, your sister is special. She has abilities that not all of us have. I suspect Kaden is after her for it." Iris finished.

"No shit, why can't any of you just tell me what the hell is going on?" Jeniva yelled, feeling that her time here wasn't very useful. She needed to find her sister, talking about how special she wasn't going to make that happen.

Christian watched the anguish on her face. He moved to the side of her and grasped her hand. Jeniva calmed at his touch and looked at him with pleading eyes.

"We don't know all the answers," Christian's voice was firm but compassionate, "but we do know this, a few months ago there was a shift. We see things, but we don't always understand the full story. We saw your parent's accident, that was the catalyst. Kaden began showing up here, asking questions just like you guys did about that night your sister was born."

"My parents were the catalyst? The catalyst for what?"

"For getting Maya here, whatever dark magick they are working on her, it's in deep." Iris jumped into the conversation.

"But how does any of this help me find my sister." Jeniva's eyes filled with tears. "If magick is pulling her away, is there some way we can use it to bring her back?"

"We can try, wait here." Iris stood and motioned for Christian to follow her.

Once they reached a small room, Iris went through her things looking for a white candle.

"What are you doing?" Christian asked.

"I want to try a return my love spell. Maybe with the two of us, we can pull her away long enough to break whatever is crossing her." Iris pulled out a white candle and other objects to get started.

"I thought that was for lovers," Christian questioned.

"It's for love, I'm using a white candle for the purest form of love, she loves her sister, she's here doing things she doesn't exactly believe in to try to find her, at this point I don't know what else to try, do you?" Her eyebrow raised as she looked at her son. Parts of Iris wished she had never gotten involved, and her son wouldn't be involved either. But she knew the biggest part of her could never fight her calling. This involved her long before she knew and it wasn't something she could walk away from, she needed to see it through to the end. She had visions of the darkness well before it arrived in New Orleans, and she had known since she was a little girl she would be called to a spiritual battle.

"No, I think you're right, let's try it." Christian began to help his mother gather her things.

"Jeniva, can you come in here please?" Iris's voice floated through the home. Jeniva hesitantly moved through the unfamiliar house into the room adjacent to the one she was in. Her steps were careful and cautious.

"Yes?" Jeniva stepped into the dimly lit room.

"Before we do this I need you to understand you have to set your intentions, if you don't believe don't waste my time." Iris pulled out a chair from the table and motioned Jeniva to have a seat. She pushed her feelings of doubt to the back of her mind. She didn't doubt her ability to complete the spell, but her confidence in Jeniva was low.

"Okay, whatever I can do to find my sister." Jeniva agreed.

"Listen carefully and do exactly as I say, concentrating only on reuniting with your sister. You must see it happening, and believe it. Trust me our will is a magick all it's on." Iris said as she placed the white candle in front of Jeniva.

Jeniva shook her head up and down, preparing herself for whatever Iris had in mind. She remembered being here with her sister, her sister was then eager and desperate for answers and she was willing to do whatever Iris asked and now Jeniva felt the same way. Jeniva fought back tears as she concentrated on her sister. This was all her fault and everything within her had to make it right.

"Hold the candle in your hand with the wick towards you," Iris reached to grab a small bottle of rose oil before continuing her instructions, "now as you hold it rub this oil from bottom to top, the candle always facing you. You must draw your sister to you, not away from you, so always in the direction towards you. Keep doing this until the candle is completely covered."

Jeniva did as she was told, apprehensively at first. Christian placed his hand on her shoulder as she rubbed the candle. His touch sent waves of energy through her.

"Next I want you to take this," Iris handed her a small knife, "and carve your sister's name into it, remember towards you, not away." She reminded her. Jeniva's hands shook as she carved the name into the candle.

"Now hold it and blow your breath into it, while you think about your sister returning to you," Christian's hands wrapped around Jeniva's and then Iris around his. "Concentrate only on finding your sister." Iris channeled all of her energy into her fingertips, wanting just as desperately to find Maya as her sister did.

The three stood in the room, all holding the candle and with a single thought, finding Maya. Iris struck a match and handed the small flame to Jeniva. "Light it."

Jeniva complied. Once the candle was lit she watched the flame burn and then turned towards the mother and son, "Now what?"

"Now, we wait."

Chapter Eighteen

aden made soft taps on the closed door, waiting for Delphine to respond. He knocked two more times and then twisted the knob to enter. She sat stoically on the bed, brushing her long hair. Something he had always noticed she did whenever she became anxious.

"Is everything all right?" He asked.

"Come in, please," She responded without turning towards him. "And close the door behind you." Kaden stepped inside and then took a seat next to her. His hand went to the small of her back as he leaned in to plant a kiss on her cheek.

"Get off me," words slid through her clenched teeth. Her eyes tightened.

"What's wrong?"

"I can smell the stench of her all over you!" Delphine turned towards Kaden, she couldn't see him, but she could feel him. Rage engulfed her as she continued, "What the hell do you think you're doing? Why isn't this completed yet? We are down to three days!" Delphine was furious with Kaden, more upset with him than he had been in years.

"You know what I'm doing. I'm doing whatever I have to do in order to save you!" Kaden jumped up and turned away from Delphine. Even though she couldn't see him, he still felt the need to hide his shame. He stared down at the floor, unable to meet her blind gaze.

"So why does saving me now involve you having sex with her?" Her words were venomous. He was absurd to think that she wouldn't see what was going on. Delphine knew him better than she knew himself. The moment he began to waiver about the ritual she suspected it.

"I...I," Kaden struggled to find his words.

"Don't even try to explain your bullshit. For months, I've been sitting rotting in this body, and you've been playing, dating, and fucking your way through life. Whatever savior complex you're dealing with, get over it. She has one purpose and one purpose only." Delphine's words were broken and scratchy. She coughed as she tried to continue but struggled to breathe. She grabbed the glass of water that she kept on the side of her bed and began to sip. "Just go, and finish this." He hesitated, wanting to console her, to let her know he was sorry for hurting her, but she was right, there was no excuse for his behavior. When it came to Maya he was torn. There was something different about her, some type of connection that he hadn't been prepared for. He looked again at Delphine, but she had turned her back to him. He shook his head as he headed towards the door. It didn't matter how different Maya was, he thought, just as Delphine had said, she had only one purpose and it was time to finish what had already been started.

Kaden left the room and saw Maya, who was entering in from the backdoor. He watched her as she folded the blanket they had just used. He was again conflicted but knew he had a task to complete. He would miss the woman he was beginning to know and had against his better judgment, he'd developed some type of feelings for. He looked back at the closed door and knew his feelings meant nothing. How do you compare a lifetime to only months?

"Maya," Kaden smiled, "why don't I let Naima and Naya take you upstairs to get cleaned up. They can give you a change of clothes and I will get dinner started."

Maya looked at him and smiled. She wanted to tell him about the message she received near the water but decided she would wait. "Okay, a bath does sound good."

Both Naya and Naima led her upstairs, neither of them speaking a word. They led her into the same room she visited the first time she was here. It again was dimly lit with candles all around the room and bed.

"Did your brother do this for me?" Maya smiled as her body filled with desire. She had never known a man like Kaden and her heart beat differently for him. She felt somehow they were destined to meet and even though this had come on the heels of extreme heartache and loss for her, Maya wouldn't take back allowing him in.

"Would you like a glass of wine?" Naima asked as she eyed Maya over her shoulder.

"Sure," Naima walked towards the bottle of wine and grabbed a glass. She waved her hand back and forth over the glass, poured the red substance into the empty container, and then handed it to Maya. Maya slowly sipped the wine, savoring its sweet taste on her tongue.

"The bathroom is right through there, we will get some clothes for you, don't worry, we got you." Naya's eyes glowed in the candlelight. Her amber brown stare glowed in the candlelight and she never taking her eyes off of Maya. Maya walked into the bathroom and closed the door. She shuffled over to the claw foot bathtub and turned on the hot water. As she undressed her body became icy cold and a wave of fear and uncertainty came over her. The room went black as she heard her sister's voice call out to her. She turned in a circle looking for her, trying to find the direction of the voice but in every corner, there was nothing there. Maya's heart raced as she turned in circles trying to make sense of what was happening. Her breaths were short and sporadic as called for help.

"Naya, Naima...I...what's happening?" Her head throbbed as her sight wavered in and out. Everything was foggy as she struggled to maintain her composure.

The girls heard the commotion in the bathroom but never moved. Maya turned in circles tripping over her own feet. The room seemed to grow, expanding into a never-ending labyrinth that she couldn't break free of. She could see shadowy crippled fingers curling towards her in the darkness. Maya scurried further and further away from the darkness that seemed to chase her. The cold porcelain tub stung her leg as she backed away, causing her to flip head first into the running warm water. Her body convulsed as she struggled to gain her balance and lift herself out. Her arms flailed as she fought the invisible force that held her in the water. The more she moved the heavier her limbs.

Time seemed to slow as she struggled to move and the room spent out of control. Maya's head slipped under the water before bouncing to the top. Her body was immobile and completely limp.

The bathroom door creaked open as Naya and Naima stood over Maya's body. Her body floated lifelessly on top of the water. The women reached into the warm water, Naya by her head and Naima at her feet and lifted her out of the tub. They laid her body on the floor and finished removing her clothes, leaving her completely nude on the floor. They went to work, washing her body from head to toe. She needed to be clean in both body and spirit.

"Go get the herbs and sage, we will start in here and once

she is prepared we can move her to the altar." Naima took charge. Once Naya returned to the room she handed her sister the sage stick and struck a match to light it.

Naima held the bundle of sage over the lit match and began to twirl it to light it on all sides. Happy with the streams of smoke that billowed from the sage, she began to sway it back and forth over Maya's body. Naya watched as the cleansing had begun. The sage would remove energies surrounding Maya.

"Go open the windows to release anything that is attached to her." Naya went around the room cracking the windows. She moved hurriedly, she was more than ready for this to be over. In her opinion, this had gone on for far too long and she was somewhat upset that Kaden had used this as an excuse to have his fun. Naya returned to the room.

Naya grabbed her feet while Naima grabbed her shoulders again and then the two lifted Maya and carried her to the bed. Once her body was in position, the women smoothed out her hair behind her and placed both hands at her side and then secured them both with restraints.

"She's ready, go and let them know we can begin," Naima exhaled and closed her eyes. Soon all this would be a distant memory and her family could finally move on.

Chapter Nineteen

Iris and Christian watched as Jeniva slept on the sofa. They insisted she stay close after casting the spell. Iris's eyes shifted toward her son.

"Can you do this?" She asked.

"I can do whatever I need to do," Christian answered while standing up. He needed to put some distance between himself and what was happening. He just needed a moment to himself. He walked out of the front door to get some fresh air.

Jeniva stirred on the sofa, her body shifting from left to right. Her legs moved restlessly as her head turned from side to side. Her body shuddered before going completely still. Her eyes flew open. Iris noticed the change in Jeniva and knew something was happening.

"Jeniva?"

"I think I know where she is, I saw her face coming towards me in a dream she was in a bathroom, then I saw the house. The house sits by itself deep in the swamp. How is any of this even possible? How did I see this?" Jeniva's head fell into her hands as she sobbed. Something was happening to her sister and she didn't know how to help her.

"Your sister is showing you, the spell we did was to bring her back to you, when we cast a spell we don't know exactly how and when it will manifest. Her abilities allow her to communicate and travel in different ways, how much can you remember of what she showed you."

"I remember she was inside a house, then the outside of a huge home that looked like it was in the middle of nowhere, and there is a long bridge across a body of water." Iris reached out her hands towards Jeniva. Jeniva just stared at Iris's outstretched hands, unsure of what she was trying to do.

"Show me," Iris grabbed Jeniva's hands and closed her eyes. She inhaled deeply and counted to ten as she released her breath. Jeniva's eyes danced from side to side, unable to focus on Iris. Iris's clammy hands held her tightly. She wanted to snatch her hands away but obliged Iris.

"I know, I know how to find her. Christiaaaaaaan." Christian appeared in the hallway, eager to find out what his mother has found out about Maya.

"Yes,"

"I know how to find her, let's go." Iris stood to her feet. "Give me the keys, it will be faster if I drive."

Jeniva reluctantly handed her the keys. Jeniva's heart pounded like a drum in her chest. She twisted her fingers in her palms trying to calm herself as she sat in the backseat watching Iris whip the car through traffic.

"How do you know where to find her?"

"I saw what she showed you, you only got bits and pieces I saw the full vision through you." Iris looked over her shoulder towards Jeniva as she spoke. Jeniva sat back in the seat and eyed the two of them. She watched as they stole glances of one another. Jeniva crossed her arms as they seem to share a secret that she didn't know.

"Seems like you guys are holding out on me, what aren't you saying." Jeniva may not have had any special abilities like her sister, but she could tell by the way they were acting something was missing from their story. The more she thought the more she realized it seemed as they were always there. "I think you know more, I mean, what do you get out of helping us so much?" Jeniva demanded answers. With so much going on she hadn't noticed it before, but they were always there, willing and ready to help. Now, she wanted to know why.

"You're the one who came to us, Jeniva. We're here because you asked us to be." Iris looked at her through the rearview mirror, readying herself for the argument she was sure Jeniva was trying to start. Jeniva rolled her eyes and sat back against the seat, trying to dismiss the distrust that was brewing inside of her. The car rolled to a stop as they reached the dead end of a long street.

"What are you doing?" Jeniva said as she looked around the dead end. "It's nothing back here."

"I know, we just passed the house, we will park here and we can come around the side of the house so we are not seen. There is no way they are just going to let us walk up to the door." Iris put the car and park and cut the car off. Jeniva opened the door and stepped out of the car, followed by the other two.

"I don't see a house," Jeniva squinted as she looked around. The only thing she saw was green grass, tall trees, and a setting sun that cast an eerie glow in the sky.

"It's through this trail," Christian pointed down a dirt path that led into the woods. Looking around the street she knew there was no way they could have seen a house from the street.

Jeniva hugged herself tightly while walking behind Iris and Christian. She moved swiftly behind the two keeping close on Christians heels. She didn't trust the old woman but at least Christian seemed okay. He helped her each and every time she called but it wasn't like she had anyone else to lean on. She cut her eyes towards Iris and exhaled. But to her, Iris was a completely different story. There was more there she wasn't telling her. Suddenly they stopped. Jeniva looked up and saw a huge dilapidated home. The shutters on the home leaned and the house looked as if it hadn't been entered in years. Long mossy branches grew up the on sides of the house. The windows looked dark and covered in dust.

"There's no way Maya is in there?" Jeniva hissed. She felt as if they were wasting her time.

"When are you going to get it through your head, nothing in this world is only what you can see?" The words shot from Iris's lips, the impatience evident in her tone. Christian placed his hand on his mother's shoulder to calm her.

"Calm down, it's no time for either one of you to get irritated. We are going to have to work together to save her." Christian paused and turned towards Jeniva, "Remember when we were on Bourbon Street? It's the same thing, you see what the spell wants you to, but for people like us, we can see what's there."

Christian reached out and grabbed Jeniva's hand. Once his hand touched hers, the old rickety house was gone and a charming country home appeared. The falling shutters were now firmly attached to the house and the grand wrap-around porch and stairs were no longer broken and falling apart.

"Hold on to me, once we get inside you will be able to see and move about the house," Christian instructed. Jeniva's eyes were wide with awe as she followed close behind him.

The three tiptoed along the dirt path towards the house. They walked carefully. It was beginning to get dark and the light from inside the house illuminated the home, the light dancing and bouncing off the walls inside.

"How do we get in?" Jeniva's voice was a whisper, the words barely audible to Iris and her son. Instead of responding Iris tipped to the house and placed her palm flatly against the wooden frame. She closed her eyes and inhaled. The side of the house was warm and radiated with energy. She inhaled and then gradually released her breath. Everything was a fog in her mind, a smoky gray haze clouded her vision. Iris slowed her breath even more, pushing out her breaths to calm herself. The protection spell on the house was strong and she was unsure if she would be able to breakthrough.

Her body flooded with heat as she as the haze in her vision intensified. Her head flew back and her eyes began to roll. Christian watched as his mother struggled to break the barrier of protection that had been placed around the house. He stepped forward and touched her shoulder, allowing his energy to flow into her. They breathed as one.

Iris, with the help of Christian, was able to gain focus, the cloudy smoke began to clear. Her head straightened, and her eyes danced back and forth, up-down and then left to right again. Iris vibrated and then became as still as a statue. Her eyes were still blank as she stared at the house. After minutes she blinked and Christian removed his hand.

"I know a way in, follow me," Iris turned her head and pointed towards the back of the house, "this is the way in."

Chapter Twenty

Maya trembled as she laid naked on the bed. Her hair had been cleansed and combed and now laid down against her shoulders. Her eyes fluttered as she struggled to open them and focus on what was happening. The last thing she remembered was running a bath before blacking out.

She pulled her hands to the side, attempting to sit up. The restraints pulled her back down against the bed. Her arms thrashed back and forth as she tried to free herself.

"Kaden! Kaden!" Maya called as she struggled to release herself from the restraints. Naya and Naima entered the room, each walking with two lit, black candles in their hands. They were silent as they walked through the room, placing the lit candles on the bed, one on each bedpost.

"Naima, let me up! Why are you doing this?" Tiny bumps of terror prickled Maya's bare skin. Naima looked down at Maya's body and rolled her eyes. Her irritation was on full display as she stared down at Maya.

"Hand me the knife," Naima stretched her hand towards Naya. Naya placed the golden dagger in her hand. Its handle was ornate and curved, etched with the same markings under the bed.

Naima bent down with the dagger in her hand and pushed it into the hardwood floor. The wood floor gave way to the pleasure of the blade, making a scratching sound as she began to etch the necessary symbols. Her hand steady, she drew a line from the first marking to the next, connecting them. As she did this, Naya went behind her. At the first post, she placed water, then the dirt from a cemetery to represent earth, the next post she lit a small candle for fire, and lastly a stick of incense to create smoke for the air. With the four classical elements represented they could begin.

"Dad," Naya shouted out the door.

"What?" Maya mumbled under her breath, her heart pounded so hard she felt as if she was near heart attack. "Let me go!" Maya screamed as loud as she could. A burst of air flooded the room. She twisted her arms and feet, trying to release her limbs from the restraints that tugged against her skin. The more she moved the tighter they seemed to get. "Let me gooooooo!"

"Shut her up!" Naima instructed. Naya walked to a dresser in the room and grabbed a black satin sash. She walked to Maya and wrapped the sash around her head and cover her mouth. Muffled sounds escaped the gag, but the sounds were hushed and unintelligible. Maya thought about the water figure that approached her, telling her to leave. Regret and fear gripped her as she desperately wished she had taken the time to listen to the ghostly figure that appeared to her only moments after Kaden had left her alone. Perhaps if she listened, her situation may be different.

Tears rolled down her cheeks. Her eyes darted from side to side as she watched the two women hover over her. *Why are they doing this?* She didn't understand what she had gotten herself into and didn't know how she would get herself out. She flopped her head against the pillow, magick was something that was new to her, she had no idea how to use it to get away. She closed her eyes, wondering why Kaden hadn't come.

Maybe I can contact him. Maya tightened her closed eyes into tiny slits as she concentrated on what Kaden had taught her. She cleared her mind and set her intention on contacting him. It had worked before without them even trying, and she was desperately trying to recreate that moment.

Kaden, can you hear me?

Maya waited, hoping he would answer. She opened her eyes. Kaden stared down at her.

"Yes, I can hear you." He smiled leaning down towards her ear. Maya was confused by his words. He stood looking down on her. Her heart broke as she realized he wasn't there to help her, he did nothing to free her, just gazed down at her naked body, making her feel more exposed than she had ever felt. "You were my favorite one," Kaden whispered and then kissed her on her cheek. He turned to face Naya and Naima. "Is everything ready?"

"Yes,"

"Kaden, what's happening?" Maya wanted answers to her questions.

"You are the vessel."

"What do you mean vessel," Her mouth was dry as she repeated the words. Vessel? Maya stared up at Kaden's soft brown eyes, she had trusted him, now she felt foolish for not listening to anyone.

"Don't feel foolish, you couldn't have fought it even if you wanted to. Root magick is strong. From the moment your binding began to unravel you were vulnerable. We just needed access to you, something to get you here so we started by removing your parents." Kaden and the women turned to leave the room,

Maya's thoughts ran rampant in her mind. She wondered what he meant by removing her parents. Her lips trembled as she remembered the vision she hadn't understood when she touched her father's things. There was a cloud of smoke that surrounded the car in her vision.

"Oh my God, they died because of me" Her voice quivered as she spoke to no one in particular. The floor creaked. Maya lifted her head and turned towards the direction of the sound. She could see Iris first and then Christian and Jeniva followed closely behind.

"Jeniva!"

"Shhhh," Iris put her finger over her lip as she moved towards the bed Maya was tied to. "Christian you untie her feet, Jeniva, help me with her hands." As they worked to release her they suddenly could not move. Their hands hovered lifelessly above the restraints.

"What are you doing, get me out so we can get the hell out of here," Maya shrieked no longer caring about how loud her voice was. She wanted to leave and didn't understand why they all stood there frozen. They looked like stone statues, still and unable to move.

"They can't move, they can only do what I allow." Kaden entered the room, holding Delphine tightly at the elbow. Delphine's old frail body was completely naked as well. Her paper thin skin was wrinkled and loose. Her breast sagged like heavy bags, stretched and thin from the weight of the years. Her legs were emaciated, her long bones appearing fragile, and unable to support her weight. She looked like walking death.

Her long hair was unbraided and hanging down to her waist, swaying as she walked. On her stomach etched in her skin was a brand of lines and symbols with a center star. Her glossy white eyes stared straight ahead as she shuffled with

Kaden's assistance towards the bed. Naya and Naima weren't far behind. When they walked into the room they held three small doll like figures in their hands.

"Poppets," Naya shook the figures in the air. "Voodoo dolls are some of the simplest forms of magick, but very effective." She took all three of the dolls and tightened the binding that was loosely around the dolls' hands. She then took a long nail and slammed it into the arm of all three dolls, nailing them to the wall.

Maya watched as her sister, Christian and Iris mimicked the action, their bodies flying back towards the walls, their arms in the exact same position as the dolls. They stood motionlessly, unable to move, and under the complete control of Naya and Naima. After they were secured to the wall, Naya and Naima helped Delphine get into the bed next to Maya.

"Wait," Delphine spoke. She had things on her mind she needed to say before they began. Everyone turned to look at her waiting for her to finish. "Maya," her mouth curved to the side as she spoke. "You wanted so desperately to know what happened to your family, well I didn't lie, they are all dead because I killed them. Your mother thought she would outsmart us?" Delphine leaned down, hovering near Maya's head. Her hot breath blazing up the side of Maya's neck. "You thought you could have what's mine? Now I will take what's been mine since the day you were born, you. And you will be nothing more than a distant memory, a tiny speck of nothing-ness, erased from existence just like your family." She coughed as the last words flew from her lips. "I'm ready now."

"Kaden, stop listen to me, please son!" Iris cried out to Kaden, her voice cracking with each word. After hearing what Delphine said, she hoped he would hear here. She pleaded for him to stop. Her heart broke as she watched in horror.

"Stop calling me that old woman, your son isn't here anymore," Kaden answered. He walked to a small metal tool shaped like the brand that was Delphine. The metal changed color as it heated, burning brighter and brighter the hotter it became.

"I know you're in there!"

"What do you mean, son?" Jeniva darted her eyes, eying both of them. The missing pieces of the puzzle were slowly falling into place for her. Christian looked at the scene around the room and felt helpless not to save his mother or brother.

"What do you mean brother?" Jeniva said again. "See I knew it, I knew you hiding something ...I...,"

"Shut up!" His voice boomed through the room, echoing throughout the house. "I'm not your son, just as I told you before, he's gone. You keep showing up thinking you can persuade me to bring him back, this is my body old lady. Your son is dead!"

"I know you're in there, I'm sorry I never should have let you go! I didn't know I had a choice in the matter, I should have fought harder like her mother."

"You didn't have a choice," Delphine sat up. "The prophecy would be fulfilled no matter what. Your family made its deal, and the bloodline bond was sealed the moment your son was born. He was always meant to be a vessel for my husband, just as my daughter's each had their designated vessels. This is the way it has been done for hundreds of years. This is the way it will continue," Delphine finished. She was tired of speaking and couldn't wait to be rid of the weak decaying body she found herself in.

"Let's begin," Kaden commanded. He walked over with the hot brand in his hand and pressed the blazing steel into Maya's skin. Maya howled in pain as her skin seared, the smell of burning flesh filled the room. The pain was so intense Maya's body went numb before everything faded to black.

Chapter Twenty-one

Everything seemed hazy to Maya as she tried to figure out where she was. She floated in a dark abyss; it was a deep chasm of nothingness. A beam of light illuminated the darkness.

"Maya," the voice floated through the air.

"Who's there?"

"It's me, your mother, Marcelle."

"Where am I?" Maya walked towards the light that shined like a beacon to a ship in the darkness. As she got closer, her mother's figure came into view. It was the same face she had seen in Seattle and in the water just hours ago. Then behind her stood her father and mother, Grace and Anthony. She rushed towards them her head falling against her father's shoulder while she slipped her hand into her mother's. Her heart swelled being in the presence of her parents. She looked at them with tears in her eyes, wondering if it wasn't for her, would they still be here?

"You're in the in-between," Grace cupped Maya's face, "we

always tried to protect you. I was a nurse at the hospital where you were born. Your mother pleaded for our help. When she touched my hand she knew how hard it had been for your father and me to conceive. She told me I was the one. At the time, I didn't understand, but when you were found alone in that cemetery, I knew we had to give you a home. And we did that. We knew we needed to protect you. So we took you as far away as we could and we never looked back." Maya listened as her mother spoke, giving her answers to some of the blank spaces in her life's history.

"I'm sorry, I know there is more you want to say, but we have very little time," Marcelle spoke up, "time passes differently in the in-between, and if you stay here too long you will get stuck. Listen carefully baby, they are planning to use you. It's the very reason I did the ritual. Unfortunately, the binding was incomplete, it unraveled and as soon as your powers began to come to fruition they could find you. I should have buried the binding, to keep your powers buried. This sacrifice is because of me."

"Use me how?" Maya's eyebrows furrowed as she waited for her to answer.

"For years our families had a pact with them. Their original names aren't even known to us, but there were four bloodlines, pure in spirit and in power. The combination of the two creates someone like you, powerful, able to master all aspects of magick, and the perfect vessel for them to pass into. They pass from body to body, moving through the centuries as different people but always of the same bloodlines." Marcelle paused to make sure that Maya was following.

"What do you mean pass," Maya stared blankly at her.

"I mean if we don't get this out of this, the woman, Delphine will pass into your body, and you will no longer exist, do you understand? I've been trying to send you signs to help you along the way. The lady you met, Christian and Iris, her son was Kaden, he was the firstborn of her bloodline and the ritual has been completed for him, as well as their daughters. Those are not his sisters. Iris attached to you, to try to protect you but she hoped you could get close enough to bring her son back to her. She thinks if she conjures a banishing spell, she can eject the spirit from her son. She's not powerful enough to do either. She's just a seer and her son is beyond being saved. But you can save yourself from the same fate, you can do this."

Maya took in all of the information that Marcelle was sharing with her. She spoke as if she really believed that Maya was strong enough to break this cycle and save them all. Maya was less confident.

"I don't think I can do this, the only thing I know about magick is what Kaden showed me and that's not a lot. So how do I save them by being able to only make a money candle or read people's minds? I can't do this, you have to help me." Maya looked at all three of them.

"Maya you can, you're stronger than you know. We only have a few more seconds, listen, you have to cleanse by fire! Use your mind to release yourself," Marcelle tapped Maya's forehead, "and the others, when you turned twenty-five your powers completely materialized. Just think it, baby, all you have to do is . . ."

Maya could feel herself being pulled backward. The light that was her family became a tiny dot in the distance and then they were gone. Marcelle's voice carried through the darkness until it was inaudible.

"Wake up!" Maya felt the slap of a hand across her face. Naya stood over her. She looked around the room at them as anger simmered inside of her. The more her Marcelle's words rang through her head the angrier she became.

"She's awake, we can start now." Kaden leaned over and kissed Delphine lightly on the lips, "Until we meet again my love."

Delphine grabbed Maya's bound hands and then Kaden began to say words Maya didn't understand.

Just use your mind

Maya heard the voice in her head. She concentrated on her sister and the others pinned to the wall. She needed to make sure that they were safe. Maya calmed her breathing and thought about how she could get them out of this. She pictured a wall in her mind, a fortress of her thoughts to keep Kaden out. After she felt confident in her wall to block Kaden, she decided to try to communicate with Christian. Given what her mother told her about Iris's true intentions of saving her son, she didn't think that Iris would listen to her, instead, so instead, she would establish a connection with Christian.

Christian, can you hear me? She looked to make sure the others weren't aware of what she was trying to do. Confident that no one knew she was speaking to him she continued.

Yes

I know how to get us out of this. I'm going to try to free you guys, when you're free you need to run like hell and get out of the house.

I can't leave my brother.

You'll have to, he's not your brother anymore, my mother came to me, she told me you guys wanted to save him, but he can't be saved.

She watched as the look of disappointment washed over his face. The sadness was evident to both of them. She understood what loss looked like, she had experienced every waking moment for the past few months.

Christian looked towards her and nodded his head. Maya began to concentrate on the dolls nailed to the wall. She visualized moving them but nothing happened. The pressure on her felt like a ton of bricks as she tried to move the nail. Finally, the nails began to spiral. They turned counter-clockwise before falling completely out of the wall. As soon as they dropped to the floor Christian, Iris, and Jeniva's bodies fell to the floor.

Maya looked at the candles around the room. One by one

she saw them falling with her mind's eye. The candles tumbled to the floor creating a blaze of fire that made a path for the three of them to exit.

"What the hell?" Naima screamed. Kaden paused for a moment and looked towards the commotion. He watched as Christian grabbed his mother's hand and told Jeniva to run.

"We don't have time, we will catch them, we have to complete this, we've already started and if we don't your mother's spirit will have nowhere to go." Kaden turned his attention back to Delphine and Maya. He looked down at Maya and noticed her eyes. They seemed to burn a bright brown. He dismissed it and focused again on his wife, unable to see the fury fueled magick she was wielding.

Maya began to focus on freeing herself. She was surrounded by people and didn't know exactly how to get out of here. She noticed Delphine's body started to shake. She didn't understand what that meant but she deduced it couldn't have been good. She thought of the ties on her feet being released first. She could feel the fabric unravel but never moved. Next, she did the ones around her arm.

"What the fuck do you think you're doing?" Kaden's voice was filled with anger as his hands wrapped around her neck. She struggled to breathe. Her hands flew to her neck as she clawed at his strong hands to try to release herself.

"I will hold her down. Naima, get over here and finish reciting the spell, Naya we will find the other's as soon as I oversee the completion of the transfer." Kaden pressed his hand further around her neck rendering her immobile. Naima stepped in and started to chant. Maya could feel her body going numb. Her legs kicked against the bed, she was desperately trying to fight for her life.

"Nooooo!" Maya's muffled voice shouted through the satin sash that was tied around her mouth. As she screamed the bed began to shake and the other four flew backward. Delphine still shook on the bed. Now free, Maya grabbed one of the black candles from the bedpost and threw it onto the bed. The bedsheets began to burn as Maya scrambled to free herself from the bed. Delphine's body shook as the flames engulfed her body.

Her clothes were in a pile at the doorway, she grabbed her dress and threw it over her body. Smoke swirled through the room as the fire grew higher and higher. Now outside of the doorway, Maya watched as the girls worked to pull Delphine from the burning bed, her feeble body, now unresponsive. Kaden stood motionless in the corner, staring at Maya. She stared back, locking eyes with him as her lips thinned into a menacing scowl. She had trusted him and he had tried to kill her.

It's not over. His voice rang loud in her head.

No Kaden you're wrong, this is done, Go to hell. Maya envisioned the flames growing higher, as soon as she did the flames fiery fingers reached for the ceiling, further engulfing the room in the treacherous fire.

"Come on," Maya jumped at the sound of Jeniva's voice, "you know I wasn't going to leave you in here, let's go!"

Maya turned around and began to run behind Jeniva. She stopped and looked back at the room before racing down the stairs. She could see all of them at the door trying to get through the flames. Christian and Iris waited for them in the kitchen.

"Come on this way," Christian called from the back door.

"Wait, I have to make sure they don't come after us," Maya quickly scanned the kitchen. She didn't feel confident enough to try to use her power to set the house on fire, instead, she walked to the stove and turned on the gas and grabbed a lighter, and lit a towel she found nearby. As soon as they were safely outside the house she through the lit towel back in.

"Run!" She screamed as they ran around the house to the

front attempting to make it to the car. Maya stopped in the driveway and looked at the fire. She needed to make sure that the house went down in flames and all of them with it. Fire billowed from the top window. She saw the window open, and a leg fall from the inside.

"Oh shit, he's getting away!" Maya tried again to concentrate, "It's not working, I can't . . ." Maya's anxiousness was causing her to lose her focus, she couldn't seem to cause the fire to grow no matter how hard she tried. Just as she was speaking a loud boom blew through the quiet night. Windows shattered sending glass and pieces of wood flying through the air. Flames engulfed the house.

"Come on let's go, there's no way they can survive that. Let's get out of here, it's over." Christian said.

All in shock, they rode in silence once back inside the car. Iris sobbed softly in the backseat next to Maya, while Jeniva was next to Christian. Maya watched and noticed the way he looked at Jeniva and smiled.

"How did you know you could do it?" Iris asked. "They are very strong, how did you do it,"

"When I passed out on the bed after the brand," Maya stopped for a moment and pulled her dress away from the newly formed brand in her side. "My parents and my mother Marcelle came to me in a vision. They told me about Kaden really being your son, the bloodline pact of both of our ancestors, and the last thing she told me was how to access my power. She said that the answer was fire," Iris shook her head up and down as she listened to Maya, tears still in her eyes.

"You know, she told me there's nothing you could have done. It was already completed. Your son wasn't there anymore. I'm so sorry." Maya reached out and grabbed Iris's hand and squeezed tightly. She appreciated the woman that had stepped in and helped her. Had it not been for her and Christian, she could have ended up just like Kaden, lost forever.

Jeniva smiled at Christian, she didn't want to admit it but he had definitely helped saved her ass. She looked over her shoulder towards her sister. Their eyes connected. Maya didn't need any words to know what she was thinking, she knew her sister loved her and had proved she would go to the ends of the earth to save her.

"You think I can finally get your ass on that plane back to Seattle?" Jeniva said jokingly but was completely serious.

"Without hesitation," Maya said as she sank back into the backseat. She couldn't wait to be back home.

Epilogue

Six Months Later

Maya kneeled outside working in the flower bed that wrapped around the porch of her parents' house that she had permanently moved into. The screen door squeaked as it opened.

"We're about to head out to a movie, you wanna join us?" Maya stood and looked at Christian and Jeniva. Jeniva leaned her head against his arm as he waited for her to answer. Through everything they had been through she was glad her sister had found some happiness. Christian went back and forth from Louisiana to Washington to see Jeniva but to also help her with being able to understand her power. Maya hadn't said anything to them, but she had already foreseen their wedding. She smiled.

"No, I think I will stay here and curl up with a book."

"Okay," Jeniva answered. It was extremely hard to get her sister out of the house, but she understood that she needed the time to herself. Even after six months, she knew Maya was still coming to grips with everything that had happened. It was easier for Jeniva to compartmentalize her feelings, she wasn't living with the pressure of harnessing growing powers like her sister. So if Maya needed time alone that is exactly what Jeniva would give her.

Maya waived bye to the pair and then cupped her growing

belly. The life growing inside of her had been unexpected, but with each passing day, she grew closer and closer to the little person her body was creating. As her hand settled on her rounded stomach, she felt a kick. She looked down at her stomach and smiled, softly singing to her unborn child. The wind blew causing her dress to dance lightly around her legs. She looked back one more time as she made her way back onto the porch.

Maya

The wind whispered her name. She turned to see no one. She shook her head and continued to the swing that hung from the porch.

From the distance he watched her lay lazily on the swing, her belly protruding with his seed. To lose everything he loved and had known for centuries in a matter of moments had devastated him. His emotions were mixed when it came to her. There was an undeniable connection he had, but she was also the cause of the death of his entire family.

He had watched her for days once he found her. Christian had taught her all about cloaking and protection, he was teaching her how to harness the power of herbs and use them for magick and rootwork.

His mouth curled into a sly smile. It didn't matter to him how many protection spells she did he would always find her. She had something that was his. He stared at her stomach. The loss of his wife and girls shattered him, but when he looked at Maya's pregnant belly, he knew he could have a family again. He knew that his line could continue. Maya would love him, he would make sure of that.

Maya felt an uneasiness wash over her. She stood and looked around the yard but didn't see anyone. She knew there should have been no way any of them survived that explosion but just in case, Maya made sure the house was protected.

She hugged her body and decided to go into the house. Just as she opened the door she heard it again.

Maya. She looked but still saw nothing. She walked into the house and locked both locks. He watched her, knowing she heard him, and just as he had done before Kaden planned to first establish mental contact with her.

"You're mine," Kaden whispered his desire to the wind before turning and walking away.

REMEMEBER TO LEAVE A REVIEW

Did you enjoy the series, remember to leave a review! Let me know what you think.

UNDISCLOSED SERIES

THE COMPLETED SERIES BOX SET

Looking for a good read? Undisclosed is a sexy series full of suspense and heat. A tangled web of lies where worlds collide and nothing is as it seems. Get Your Copy Today

ABOUT THE AUTHOR

DeiIra Smith-Collard is an author from Houston, Texas. With a creative writing style that intertwines fact with fiction, love and lust, and moral dilemmas, her books are thought to challenge the mind and question the lines of relationships, love and life.

DeiIra's first novel, Love Lust & a Whole Lotta Distrust was self-published in 2008 and met with great reviews. After the success of the first novel, DeiIra went on to write for Anexander Books, publishing her next 2 full length novels, Secrets, Sins and Shameful Lies and Role Play. In addition to her full length novels, she has also published a short story, My Extra and was also featured in 3 anthologies, Bedtime Stories ,Coffee Confessions and Love Never Fails.

In addition to writing DeiIra Smith-Collard is also the Founder and Editor-In-Chief for Le Charme Magazine and a freelance photographer/graphic and web designer.

Text GETLIT to 66866 for updates, giveaways and more!
www.deiirasmithcollard.com
info@deiirasmithcollard.com

STAY CONNECTED

Text GETLIT to 66866 for new releases, giveaways and reader giveaways

ALSO BY DEIIRA SMITH-COLLARD

LOVE & LUST SERIES

Love Lust and A Whole Lotta Distrust

Secrets Sins & Shameful Lies

UNDISCLOSED SERIES

Undisclosed:A Tale of Love And Deceit

Undisclosed 2: A Tale of Obsession and Revenge

Undisclosed 3: A Tale of Passion and Betrayal

Full Disclosure: A Tale of Revelation And Resentment:

Undisclosed: The Completed Series: Books 1-4

STAND ALONES

The Games We Play

My Extra: Short Story (Free Read)

Broken Pieces: Short Story (Free Read)

www.ingramcontent.com/pod-product-compliance
Lightning Source LLC
Chambersburg PA
CBHW051845170626
46807CB00003B/1361